Myron's laughter filled the kitchen. Suddenly his hands closed around Kerri's waist and she felt herself lifted in the air. Then she was in his arms and his lips sought hers. Her pulse quickened as he held her tighter and kissed her with a demanding pressure that both excited and frightened her.

A sound broke the spell. Kerri started and pulled away, her face flaming. She was shaken by her conflicting feelings.

Derrick was standing by the door. "Excuse me," he said coldly. "I didn't mean to interrupt you." Turning on his heel, he left before Kerri had a chance to say a word.

Dear Readers,

We at Silhouette would like to thank all our readers for your many enthusiastic letters. In direct response to your encouragement, we are now publishing *four* FIRST LOVEs every month.

As always FIRST LOVEs are written especially for and about you—your hopes, your dreams, your ambitions.

Please continue to share your suggestions and comments with us; they play an important part in our pleasing you.

I invite you to write to us at the address below:

Nancy Jackson
Senior Editor
Silhouette Books
P.O. Box 769
New York, N.Y. 10019

CHANGE
PARTNERS
Sharon Wagner

First Love from Silhouette
Published by Silhouette Books New York
America's Publisher of Contemporary Romance

SILHOUETTE BOOKS, a Division of Simon & Schuster, Inc.
1230 Avenue of the Americas, New York, N.Y. 10020

Copyright © 1983 by Sharon Wagner

Distributed by Pocket Books

ISBN: 0-671-53368-1

First Silhouette Books printing October, 1983

10 9 8 7 6 5 4 3 2 1

America's Publisher of Contemporary Romance

Printed in the U.S.A.

To my mother, Dorothy Wagner,
who not only helped, but believed,
with thanks and love.

1

Kerri McGuire turned from the window with a sigh. Spring had come late to Spokane, Washington, this year; but now at the end of May, everything was blooming—everything but her life.

"It won't be that bad, Kerri," her grandmother said from the kitchen stove where she was checking on the progress of dinner. "You like Bob, don't you?"

Kerri shrugged. "He's okay, I guess," she admitted grudgingly.

"He's made your mother very happy."

"Big deal." Kerri returned her attention to the profusion of roses and lilacs beyond the glass. Her grandmother had lived in the same house for forty-five years and had tended her garden for all of that time.

"Your father has been dead for six years, Kerri. Don't you think that your mother deserves a chance to have a life that's more than working and taking care of you?"

The words were barbs, and at sixteen, Kerri knew that there was only one answer she could make without sounding like a selfish, ungrateful brat. But at the same time, she couldn't help feeling resentful. She didn't mind her mother having a new life; was, in fact, glad that she was happy. What hurt was realizing that the price was her own life here in Spokane.

"What about it, Kerri?" her grandmother pressed. "Are you going to mope around after your mother gets here?"

Kerri sighed. "I'm happy, I'm happy!" She blinked back her tears and fled to her room on the second floor of the old house.

Her phone rang almost immediately. Kerri picked up the receiver, trying not to remember that it had been a Christmas present from Bob Harriman, her new stepfather. The voice who answered her hello was Donna, her best friend.

"She isn't there yet?" Donna asked.

"I'm still waiting," Kerri acknowledged.

"I don't suppose you can come over tonight." Donna's tone was depressed.

Kerri simply sighed.

"But you will come over tomorrow afternoon for the farewell party? Jamie is going to be here."

Kerri fought back a sob. It wasn't fair. For two years she'd been trying to get Jamie Palmer to notice her, to realize that she was alive. And now that he'd actually talked to her . . .

"Kerri, couldn't you just stay through the summer?" Donna asked. "You could stay with me part of the time. I know Mom wouldn't care. All of us have so many things planned."

"Don't." Kerri groaned. It was a discussion they'd had a thousand times during the past few months, and she knew that Donna was as aware as she that there could be no change in the outcome. "The agreement was that I could finish my sophomore year here," Kerri managed. "School closed last week."

"So you have to go to Montana." It wasn't a question.

"Hey, you'll be coming to visit me," Kerri reminded her.

"It won't be the same after you leave," Donna continued, unconvinced.

Kerri thought of all the promises her mother had made: her own room at the resort that was located on Whitefish Lake just to the west of Glacier Park in northern Montana; her choice of the horses available for the dude-ranch guests; and a summer job that would pay her much better than the baby-sitting she'd always done. None of it made up for the loneliness she could see ahead.

"Kerri, Kerri, your mother is here." Her grandmother's voice broke through the pain of her thoughts.

"I gotta go," Kerri told Donna. "I'll call you back later, okay?"

"If you can get away tonight . . ." Donna left the invitation open as they ended the conversation.

Kerri hung up, then went over to the mirror, studying her reflection for a moment before she went downstairs. She'd been sixteen for only three weeks, and so far she couldn't see any changes at all. Her wiry auburn hair still curled too much in the damp air and her nose was already dusted with freckles from the spring sunshine. Her hazel eyes were rebellious and slightly reddened from unshed tears.

There was a sound of hurrying footsteps on the stairs. As Kerri opened her bedroom door, she was swept into her mother's arms. "Oh Kerri, I've missed you so much!" The hug was so tight that Kerri could hardly breathe; yet it felt good, and Kerri knew that she'd missed her mother, too, very much.

"I was on the phone," she managed to gasp. "That's why I didn't get downstairs."

"You look so grown up," her mother went on, pushing Kerri to arm's length to study her. "I feel like I left a little girl and came back to find a young lady."

Kerri giggled through the tears that now washed down her cheeks. "It's only been five months," she told her mother.

"Funny how it only seemed like five years," her mother answered.

"You look different too," Kerri informed her, realizing that it was true.

"Probably neglect," her mother teased. "We've been so busy getting everything ready for the season that I haven't had time to do anything for myself."

Kerri's smile froze at the mention of the dude-ranch resort. "It seems to agree with you," she muttered, turning away.

"You're going to love it, Kerri," her mother continued. "You're really lucky, you know. I saw all the job applications that Bob got from the local high-school kids. Most of them want to work at Lakeside, and we only have need for about eight, four boys and four girls."

Kerri said nothing. She'd heard it before—all about how she'd have lots of new friends right at the resort. It didn't make up for all the friends she'd be leaving behind.

"Most of the kids you'll be working with will be a

couple of years older than you, since Bob mainly hires the new graduates. They like working there because they make money for college expenses and the job is the right length of time. Our season more or less ends with Labor Day, and then they're free to go off to college."

"They all go to college?" Kerri didn't hide her disappointment.

"Most of them," her mother admitted. "But they're all from Whitefish. That's the town on the lake. That's what is so nice: They can live at home while they work for us, so we don't have to provide rooms for them. It'll be nice for you, too. Once you make friends, you'll be going into Whitefish with them and you'll make other friends who will be going to school with you in the fall. It's a small town, Kerri. You'll know everybody before you've been there a month."

Kerri swallowed an unpleasant observation, moving away from her mother to the window. "When do we have to go?" she asked.

"As soon as possible. Have you packed?" Her mother looked around.

"I really haven't had time," Kerri protested, knowing that it wasn't true. "I'll start tomorrow."

"I'll help you and we can start tonight," her mother corrected, her brown eyes meeting Kerri's hazel ones in a way that told Kerri she'd seen through the ruse. "You can stay for tomorrow's farewell party, but we'll be leaving the next morning—packed or not. There's too much to do out at the ranch for me to be gone any longer."

Kerri nodded, swallowing a sigh. "Donna's having some of the kids over tonight, too," she began, feeling guilty, yet angry at the unfairness of her world.

To her surprise, the brown eyes didn't reflect any

anger. Her mother reached out and touched her cheek lightly. "I'd like an evening alone with Mom," she said. "If you'll get right to your packing and make a real dent in it by dinner, you can go to Donna's. Just make it an early evening, promise?"

"Oh, Mom." Kerri hugged her mother, both happy and sad. In some ways the move would have been easier to bear if she could've hated her mother or Bob Harriman; their very kindness and consideration made her feel guilty for her resentment.

Both parties were fun. They had danced and talked in the evening; then the next afternoon there were hamburgers and hot dogs cooked on the backyard grill. And they danced on the wide back patio. Still, it was a bittersweet time for Kerri.

Everything that happened had the added weight of being the last time: the last evening she'd spend at Donna's house, the final afternoon of her life in Spokane. She might return for a visit, but it would never be the same.

"Drive you home?" Jamie asked that last afternoon as the farewell party came to an end. "It's on my way."

Kerri looked up at him, hardly able to breathe. He would be a senior in the fall, and he was the star of the football team and president of his class. He'd even been king of the Junior Prom last winter. Of course, at the time he'd been dating Priscilla Parnell, the queen, but now that they'd broken up . . .

"I . . . I'd like that," Kerri whispered.

"You ready to go?" His dark eyes were challenging.

"I just have to say good-bye to Donna," Kerri told him, eager to tell her friend about the invitation.

"I'll wait in the car," Jamie said, moving away from

her, his wide shoulders looking so strong even without the padding of his football gear.

"What's up?" Donna asked the moment Jamie disappeared around the side of the house. "Did he ask you out? I saw you two dancing several times, so I . . ."

"How could I go out with him?" Kerri wailed. "I leave at dawn tomorrow."

"I forgot," Donna acknowledged with a sigh. "So what is going on?"

"He's going to drive me home." The joy she'd felt at the invitation faded as the reality of tomorrow overshadowed it, spoiling the magic of the moment.

"Hey, that's neat. Maybe he'll want to write or something."

Kerri hugged Donna. "Thanks for the party," she told her, "and I'll call you as soon as we get settled and I can set a date for you to come, okay?"

"I can hardly wait," Donna assured her. "I'll bet everything will be terrific."

"Sure." They both blinked back tears as Kerri started around the house to where Jamie had parked his car. Donna went back to join the rest of her guests.

The radio was playing loudly as she slipped into the car. Jamie merely grinned at her, saying nothing. He pulled out of the driveway and turned left, away from her house, which was only two blocks from Donna's. Kerri opened her mouth to tell him, then closed it again, not wanting the moment to end.

"Guess you must be feeling pretty good," Jamie said once the song ended.

"What do you mean?" Kerri asked, startled.

"I'd sure like to be moving to a place like that,"

Jamie told her. "Horses to ride, boats, a big lake. There's even a ski resort there. We went through once on our way to Glacier Park, and it's neat."

"Well, sure, but . . ." Kerri tried to put her feelings into words, but everything that came to mind sounded like a complaint. "I'll just miss everybody," she murmured at last.

"You can always come to visit."

"It's not the same as going to school here," Kerri reminded him.

Jamie said nothing, driving easily through the streets.

"Do you think you'll be coming over that way again sometime?" Kerri asked after several minutes.

Jamie shrugged. "I might go to college over there. I've been getting catalogs from all the colleges and universities in the area—Washington, Oregon, Idaho and Montana." He grinned at her. "My grades aren't too terrific, so I thought I'd better get an early start."

"Hey, it would be fun if you were going to school in Missoula," Kerri said. "I mean, that's not too far from Whitefish."

"It's too bad you aren't going to be here this summer," Jamie went on, almost as though he hadn't heard her. "I mean, we've had a good time the last couple of days, haven't we?"

Kerri nodded, her heart suddenly pounding hard. She and Donna had talked about dating for hours, but except for double dates, she'd never really been out with anyone—at least, not with anyone like Jamie.

"I . . . I'm supposed to work for my stepdad this summer," she murmured. "At the resort."

"You're lucky to have a job," Jamie observed. "I've been hunting the last couple of weeks, and all the good ones are already filled. I don't know what I'll be doing this summer."

"It's too bad you don't live in Whitefish," Kerri told him. "That's where all the resort employees come from."

They drove up and down more streets. Kerri tried to look out the window, to be cool, but her entire attention was focused on the boy beside her. She tried to think of something to say, but no words came. She wanted to giggle and cry at the same time. She wanted the ride to go on forever, yet she longed to be home away from the feeling of helpless failure that was beginning to stalk her now that she couldn't think of anything to say.

"When you get there, you might talk to your stepdad about a job for me," Jamie continued. "I mean, if not working for him, maybe he'd know of something in the area. I have some cousins living out there that I could stay with if I could find a good job."

"I'll ask my mom," Kerri told him, her happiness growing as she realized that she might be able to continue the shy feelings that seemed to be developing between her and Jamie. "She might know of something even now."

"Do you think she'd talk to me?" Jamie asked.

"Sure. She's at my grandmother's." Kerri felt a mixture of happiness and disappointment as Jamie immediately turned the car onto a street that would take them to her grandmother's house.

Kerri introduced Jamie to her mother with a glow of pride, but her heart sank when her mother's expression changed after she mentioned Jamie's problem.

Her mother shook her head. "I really think you'd have a better chance of finding a job here, Jamie," she said. "Bob had two dozen applications from high-school senior boys, and only four jobs to fill. And the rest of the resorts are about the same."

"But there should be something," Kerri protested, afraid of never seeing Jamie again.

"I doubt it, honey," her mother contradicted.

"Well, it was a good thought," Jamie told her. "I guess I'll just have to keep looking here." He turned toward the door.

Kerri followed him reluctantly, aware that he was leaving and the magic moment was ending. "I'm sorry, Jamie," she said. "It would have been fabulous to have you in Whitefish. I mean . . ."

Jamie took her hand, his fingers rough and warm against her nerve-cold flesh. "I'd like to be there with you too," he said. "I feel sort of cheated. I mean, up until yesterday I didn't really know you. And now that I do . . ."

"We can write," Kerri suggested shyly.

"Yeah, sure. Okay," Jamie replied. "And I'll see you when you come back for visits and maybe in a year or so if I go to Missoula to school." He let it trail off.

They stood at the door just looking at each other, a lot of unsaid words filling the air between them. Finally he shrugged, then leaned forward, his lips brushing hers lightly. "See you around," he said; then he was gone.

Kerri sagged against the door, too shocked to move, then slowly she lifted her fingers to her lips. He'd kissed her. . . . Jamie Palmer had actually kissed her! She was the happiest and saddest girl in the whole world.

"Kerri, I need you in the basement," her mother called from the back of the house. "There are three boxes of your things down there and I need to know if there's anything in them that you want to take."

"I can't go now!" The words came to her lips in a rush, but she only whispered them as she looked around at the boxes that were already stacked in the front hall, at the suitcases packed and waiting. Tears filled her eyes, and she could hardly see as she went obediently to the basement.

"Wake up, sleepyhead," Kerri's mother said as they left the outskirts of Spokane and moved onto the highway. "You're starting a new life."

"I liked the old one," Kerri grumbled.

"He was a cute boy," her mother said, "but you'll meet someone just as attractive in Whitefish. In fact several of the boys who'll be working for us are just as nice-looking." She laughed. "I checked that out while we were interviewing."

"Oh, Mom." It was a groan. "You didn't tell them a bunch of stuff about me, did you?"

"Come on, Kerri. I wouldn't do that." Her mother became serious. "I mean, people know that I have a daughter and that we were just waiting for the end of the school year to have you come to live with us, but that's all."

"I just don't want to meet a bunch of new people," Kerri complained. "I wish we could have hired Jamie. He's so great. I tried all winter to get him to notice me, and finally at Donna's party . . ." She let it trail off, the pain too great to express. "He really likes me."

"Of course he does," her mother said. "Why wouldn't he?"

Kerri couldn't think of an answer. They rode in silence for a while. Finally, Kerri began to feel the strain. "What is it like?" she asked, trying to sound casual. "Lakeside, I mean."

"Well, mostly it's beautiful," her mother answered. "The lake is a big one and there's forest all around and some mountainous parts on the north shore. The ranch is quite a way from town, along the flatter part of the lakeshore."

"Is it a real ranch, or just a resort?" Kerri was intrigued in spite of herself. Her mother had written about the place from the time Bob had taken her there after their New Year's Day wedding, but the words had meant no more to Kerri than a sentence of exile.

"It was a real, working cattle ranch once," her mother explained, "but it wasn't making much money, so Bob decided to convert it. He built a beautiful two-story log lodge on the lakeshore part of the property, and there are a half-dozen smaller cabins back in the trees."

"And we'll be living in the lodge?"

"There's an owner's apartment in the back—two bedrooms with a small living room. We'll stay there during the season, but in the fall there's a much more private place away from the lake and near the main highway. That's the old ranch house. We've been living there till just recently."

"You mean, you move spring and fall?" Kerri couldn't believe her ears.

"Well, unless we decide to convert to a year-round resort and cater to the skiing crowd in the winter, we couldn't afford to heat the lodge. It was closed up all winter."

"Are you saying you don't work all winter?" Kerri

frowned. "Then why couldn't we live in Spokane in the winter? Grandma would have let you have her house, and I wouldn't have had to leave all my friends." The last was almost a wail.

"We work in the winter," her mother replied, "but not at the lodge. Bob and the Petersons run cattle, and we have to take care of them in the winter since the Petersons take them through the summer. Then, of course, there are the horses to take care of, and Bob does rent out some of the cabins to skiing parties."

Kerri lapsed into silence, unable to argue but still feeling that things could have been arranged differently if her mother really cared. She closed her eyes, not wanting to think about the ranch-resort or the life she would be leading there. It wouldn't be Spokane, she knew, and there wouldn't be anyone there like Jamie.

"You'll like the Petersons," her mother went on, seemingly oblivious to Kerri's depression. "They have a boy, Derrick, about your age; and a girl, LuAnn, who is fifteen. They're our nearest neighbors and they both help Bob with the horses. . . ."

Kerri turned her face to the window, refusing to respond to her mother's obvious attempt to interest her. Country kids, she thought bitterly. All they'd care about were cattle and horses, and they wouldn't know anything about real living.

"Bob has been checking all the horses," her mother began again. "He's picked out about a dozen for you to try."

"I thought you said I could have any horse I wanted," Kerri snapped.

"Well, you can, I suppose. Bob was just trying to

find the best ones. Some of them are for real beginners, and there are a few that only an experienced
rider can handle, so . . ."

"So who cares?" Kerri lapsed into misery, trying to
remember just how Jamie had looked when they'd
stood at the door, just how his lips had felt in the
moment when they touched hers.

Her mother sighed and said nothing till she slowed
down and pulled into a small roadside diner. "How
about some more breakfast?" she suggested. "I think
we were both too excited to eat much this morning."

Kerri just shrugged, trying to ignore the growling of
her stomach as her nose caught the scent of bacon and
pancakes. She knew that her mother was feeling bad
too, but she didn't care. Right or wrong, it was her
mother's fault that she might never see Jamie again,
and nothing about Lakeside or her "wonderful new
life" could make up for that.

When they were nearly through with big platters of
pancakes and bacon and eggs, her mother leaned back
and sipped her coffee. "I'm sorry you're unhappy,
Kerri," she said, "but there's nothing I can do about
that. If it was in my power, you know that I'd make
you happy, but it isn't."

"You could have left me in Spokane." The words
came out without her wanting them to.

"Mother is too old to wrestle with that big house
through another winter or two. She only stayed after
Dad died because she wanted to make a home for us.
I couldn't ask her to stay any longer and I couldn't ask
Bob to move there now that he's finally making a
success of his resort."

"Two more years," Kerri protested. "I could have
finished high school in two more years."

"In two years you'll be a part of another graduating

class. The kids from Whitefish are nice, Kerri, at least the ones I've met are. Give them a chance and give yourself a chance, too. I can't make you happy or make this a good change in your life, but you can. All you have to do is try."

Kerri said nothing, glaring down at her plate, no longer hungry. The thought of what lay ahead took her appetite away and made her stomach knot so that she was sure she couldn't swallow anything more. New people, new places, a whole new life—How could her mother think that she could handle it? How would she even endure the days and weeks till she could invite Donna to come out for a visit?

Her mother opened her mouth to say something else, then just sighed and began digging in her purse for her wallet. "If you aren't going to eat any more, we might as well be on our way," she said at last. "I'd like to get into Whitefish early and give you a real chance to see the town and the lake before we go on to the resort."

Kerri didn't bother to answer, unsure that she could speak around the lump in her throat. It was, she decided, going to be the longest and the worst day of her life.

2

It was midafternoon when Kerri's mother slowed, and pointed to the pretty town ahead. "That's it," she said. "Whitefish the town, and beyond it you can see the beginning of the lake. Isn't it beautiful?"

Kerri said nothing, noticing how small the town appeared, though at the moment the streets were fairly crowded. There were teenagers on the streets, she realized, most of them clad in shorts or faded jeans and T-shirts. Did they belong here, or were they tourists?

"That's the high school," her mother continued, leaving the center of town and driving up the shady side streets. "You'll have to ride the bus unless Derrick Peterson gets his car before school starts. If he does, you and LuAnn will probably ride with him."

"Ride the bus?" Kerri groaned. "Gross."

"It's not that far, really," her mother went on. "It's just that when the storms are bad and the snow is deep . . ." Her mother slowed and turned into a supermarket parking lot. "I'm going to call Bob and see if I should pick up anything," she said. "When you live on the far end of the lake, you don't run down to the store for one or two items."

Kerri didn't move.

"Don't you want to come inside?" her mother asked.

"I'll wait."

Kerri sensed that her mother was considering arguing, but after a moment she simply sighed and picked up her purse, leaving Kerri without a word. Kerri sighed too, glaring out the window at the ranks of cars that were already in the market parking lot. The afternoon was hot and the sun baked down, making the car almost unbearable.

Twisting and squirming didn't help, and after a moment Kerri surrendered and got out. Should she go inside? she wondered, sure that the store would be air-conditioned.

"Hi." A voice came from behind her. "You must be Kerri."

Kerri turned at once and looked up into friendly brown eyes. "Hi," she murmured dubiously, not sure that she should be speaking to a stranger even though he appeared to be about her age.

"I'm Derrick," he stated, waited a moment, then added, "welcome to Whitefish."

"Thanks," Kerri answered without enthusiasm, trying to remember what her mother had said. Was this the boy from the next ranch? The one she was supposed to like? She had the feeling he was.

"Where's your mother?" he asked.

"She went inside to call Bob to see if we were supposed to get some groceries," Kerri supplied, deciding that he really wasn't too bad. He was about the same height as Jamie, but slimmer; his tanned arms were strong and muscular. Black hair fell across his forehead, and he pushed it back impatiently, grinning at her.

"He won't need anything," he told her. "I just picked up the order for Lakeside." He looked over his shoulder and Kerri saw the pickup with Lakeside Resort painted on the door. "I'd better get it back out there," he continued. "See you later, Kerri."

"Sure, see you." Kerri watched him walk away, feeling a touch of depression. She'd acted like a nerd, she decided. He was nice and he'd tried to be friendly, and she'd just stood there like a dumb stick.

Her mind was suddenly filled with memories of yesterday with Jamie, and she had to blink back tears. Derrick didn't matter, she told herself coldly. He wasn't Jamie Palmer, so what did it matter what he thought about her?

"Kerri, was that Derrick you were talking to?" Her mother's voice broke into her thoughts.

Kerri turned, nodding. "I guess he recognized the car," she said.

"He's a nice boy, isn't he? I just know you'll enjoy being with him and with LuAnn."

Kerri looked at the small sack. "Bob leave something off the list?" she asked.

"What?" Her mother looked confused.

"Derrick said that he'd come in for the Lakeside supplies," Kerri explained.

"I just picked up some candy and nuts for Bob," her mother said, putting the sack in the back. "Ready for more of the tour?"

"I don't care," Kerri muttered, getting back into the car. "Whatever you want."

"We'll drive out the long way, follow the lake," her mother decided. "It's lovely but cold. Bob tells me that it never really gets warm."

Kerri listened, but said nothing as her mother pointed out the scar on the mountainside that was the Big Mountain ski area. She saw the various resorts along the lakeshore where tourists were already swimming or boating. Many of them were teenagers, and she felt a stirring of envy, realizing that she would love to change places with them. Coming here for vacation would be fun; living here was something else.

Finally, her mother seemed to give up. She stopped pointing things out and simply drove along a dusty gravel road that twisted and turned through the forest, giving occasional glimpses of the deep blue lake. At every crossroad, Kerri noted the signs pointing ahead to the Lakeside Resort. Her future was suddenly frighteningly at hand.

"Well, here we are," her mother announced, turning between log fence posts and driving toward a huge, handsome log building. "That's the lodge ahead, and you can see the stable, the corrals and three of the cabins. Over there and behind that big old pine and up on that outcropping." She pointed the cabins out for Kerri.

Kerri caught her breath. "Wow! That's really something."

"Just the way I felt," her mother told her, parking at the side of the building, then reaching out to put an arm around Kerri's shoulders. "And I saw it with two feet of snow all around."

Kerri giggled in spite of herself. "This would be a neat place for a vacation," she admitted.

"Well, you have exactly two days for that," her mother told her. "That's how long we have before our first guests arrive. Once they are here, I'm afraid our vacation is over till after Labor Day."

Kerri's euphoria faded. "I'm really going to work here?" she asked. "It isn't just something you made up?"

"Are you kidding? You'll have to work. Bob only hired three girls this year, and he usually takes four. You'll be the youngest, I'm afraid, but two of the girls are only seventeen and one of the boys is too. So it shouldn't be too bad. Also, Derrick is just sixteen, so . . ." She let it trail off.

"Derrick works here full-time?" Kerri asked.

"He has for several years. He's Bob's head wrangler now, in spite of being so young. He's really terrific with horses, and he's not bad at teaching the guests to ride, either. He'll be able to give you some pointers, too, I'm sure."

"I know how to ride," Kerri snapped, remembering clearly that for most of the years she was growing up, she'd wanted a horse of her own. But she'd never been able to have one—not till now, when she'd prefer to move on to more grown-up things.

"Well, riding at a riding academy is a little different than riding out here, Kerri," her mother began. "And some of the horses—"

"Hey, welcome to Lakeside, Kerri." Bob came around the house, a big grin lighting his dark brown eyes. When Kerri stepped out of the car, he picked her up and hugged her with the same warmth that he'd shown to her from the beginning.

Kerri, unable to resist his kindness, hugged him back, thinking again that it would make life simpler if she could hate Bob and everything he'd done to her life.

"So what do you think of the place?" he asked,

setting her back on her feet so that he could take her mother in his arms for a slightly longer embrace.

"It's really fabulous," Kerri admitted.

"Well, let's get you unloaded, then I'll give you a quick tour. You show her where her room is, Alice, and I'll start getting things out of the car, all right?"

"Grab something, Kerri," her mother ordered, picking up one of the smaller suitcases herself. "No point in going empty-handed."

Somehow the sheer work of unloading and unpacking eased the first uncertain minutes of her arrival, and by the time everything was in and spread around the sunny room, it looked almost homelike. Her mother stood in the middle of the braided rag rug that covered most of the hardwood floor and looked around.

"I thought this room was going to be big enough," she observed, shaking her head, "but now I'm not so sure. I think I underrated your pack-rat tendencies."

Kerri giggled. "Well, Bob did say we could put the overflow back in the boxes and take them to the ranch house," she reminded her. "In fact, I'm beginning to think having two houses might be all right."

"But you do like the room?" Her mother's gold-flecked brown eyes were serious.

"How could I not like it?" Kerri asked, looking around at the bright green print curtains and matching bedspread as they glowed against the golden pine walls. "It's terrific, Mom, you know that."

"I want you to be happy, Kerri."

Kerri looked up, feeling again the painful closeness that she and her mother had forged during the many bad times after her father's death in a plane crash. "I know that, Mom," she admitted. "And I will try, I promise."

The hug made her feel better, and when Bob called them to come out, she even managed a smile. "How about a tour of the property?" Bob asked. "I'd like to show you around the place, give you an idea what to expect before the thundering herd arrives."

"The what?" Kerri asked.

"Your co-workers," Bob answered. "I've invited them out for a barbecue tonight. Give you a chance to get acquainted before you have to start working with them." He grinned. "That's what Derrick was doing in town, picking up supplies for tonight."

"You did invite the Petersons, didn't you?" her mother asked.

"Certainly. I have to show off my new girl, don't I?" Bob laughed. "Now, come on. All the horses are in, so you can look over the herd and maybe spot the ones you want to try out tomorrow."

"Tomorrow?" Kerri felt a twinge of something between joy and pain.

"Well, I think you should try to see some of the trails before you have to ride out with a party of guests. Can't have you getting lost, you know."

"I'll be taking out riders?" Kerri asked, not sure how to feel about that prospect.

"If you want to. Most of the young people who work here ride, so they alternate going on the daily rides. We never send any rides out with less than two staff members, and quite often we send three. Derrick is the only one who goes all the time—He's our wrangler."

"What else will I be doing?" Kerri asked, realizing that, in her passion to not think about the future, she'd never asked her mother.

"Well, let's see. Girls are responsible for cleaning and changing all the rooms and cabins; boys take care of the outside work—the grounds, the boats, keeping the trails cleared, that sort of thing. Everybody helps with meals, serving and cleaning up. And everyone works on the various activities: setting up outings, the rides, arranging boat trips and guiding them."

"Sounds like quite a job," Kerri admitted.

"You'll be busy," Bob agreed, "but you'll have time for fun, too. We share a lot of the activities. I mean, just because you pack the picnic basket doesn't mean you won't enjoy the food, does it?" He paused and his eyes met hers with understanding. "I think you'll like being busy," he added. "You won't have so much time to miss your friends in Spokane."

Kerri winced, but she said nothing as he led her out through the large and very efficient-looking kitchen and across the shaggy grass to the bulk of the stable. A network of corrals surrounded the stable, and there were horses in three of the pens.

"Oh, wow," Kerri gasped, her unhappiness fading as the mixture of black, bay, brown, gray and white horses shifted and came over to the fence to stare back at her. "They're all gorgeous."

Bob laughed. "Derrick and I have been separating them all week," he explained. "Now, I don't know how well you ride, but we try to sort the horses according to the ability of the riders. The horses in this corral are for beginners." He waved a hand at a selection of sleepy-looking beasts. "They're extremely gentle and well trained."

"I think I'm beyond that," Kerri said at once. "I've had riding lessons for years—ever since I was about seven or eight. I haven't ridden too much this past year, but I'm sure once I get started—"

"Then you'd probably do well to pick a mount from this group," Bob told her. "That bay is a good, steady horse, and the buckskin mare is nice, too. They have enough spirit to keep you awake, but they won't hurt you."

The horses came over to the fence, and Kerri rubbed a couple of the soft noses, overcome by her choices. A whinny came from the final pen, where about a dozen horses milled around. Kerri looked over and spotted the dainty pinto at once.

Black and white spots spread regularly over the compact body, and a precise stripe of white came down the narrow head to end between the flaring nostrils. The mare crossed the corral, leaving the other horses, and came over to look at Kerri with soft, dark eyes.

"She's beautiful," Kerri said, leaving the other horses to go over and stroke the velvety muzzle. "I want her."

"That's Sky Writer," Bob said, his expression changing.

"What an unusual name," Kerri exclaimed. "She's so sweet."

"She's an unusual horse," Bob began. "I bought her because she seemed so gentle, but she's just not trustworthy, Kerri. I've been thinking about selling her."

Kerri stopped rubbing the mare's nose and turned her attention to her stepfather. "What do you mean?" she asked. "You said I could have any horse I wanted to ride, and I want her. Please don't sell her."

"Honey, she's quite a handful for an experienced rider. Outside of Derrick or LuAnn, nobody has ridden her for at least a year, and she left LuAnn out on the trail once last year."

Kerri looked at the horse, melting as the mare nuzzled her arm. Sky Writer seemed to relax as Kerri rubbed and scratched her shiny hide. "She wouldn't do that to me," Kerri crooned to the mare. "She's just going to be perfect, I know it."

Bob said nothing, but when Kerri stole a glance at him, she could see that he wasn't happy. "I really am a pretty good rider," she assured him. "And I promise I'll be careful."

He shrugged. "A promise is a promise, but if you change your mind, don't hesitate to ask for another horse. Very few people ride the same horse for the whole season, so . . ." He let it trail off. "Want to go down and see the boats and the shore?" he asked.

Kerri gave the mare a final pat, then followed him away from the corrals. She felt a twinge of guilt at defying Bob, but when she looked back, the mare was still watching her. She couldn't help feeling that they had a special bond. After all, Sky Writer was obviously a misfit, too.

By the time Kerri had admired the lakeshore sand and the new concrete pier that extended off to the deeper side of the small cove that served the resort, it was getting late and she was perfectly happy to go back to the lodge to bathe and change for the evening's party.

When she emerged from the small bath that opened off her room, Kerri found her mother waiting. "Thought you might like something new to wear," she said. "Hope this fits all right. I think you've grown a little since I saw you last."

The dress was a simple peasant style with an elasticized neck that could be worn on or off the shoulders and a full-tiered skirt all in green-and-white checked gingham. White lace frosted the neck, the short sleeves and the lowest tier of the skirt.

"Oh, it's darling," Kerri gasped, holding it up to herself as she looked in the mirror. "And it will be perfect tonight, won't it? I mean, I didn't have anything but jeans to wear."

Her mother laughed. "I've made you several, honey. They are almost a uniform here. Jeans and western shirts during the day, gingham dresses in the evenings or for dances."

"Gosh, thanks," Kerri murmured. "It's really neat."

"Well, I had plenty of time earlier this spring, so I did quite a lot of sewing. Now, hurry and get dressed and you can help me carry the food out to the terrace. That's where we'll be eating." Her mother twirled on one toe, giving her own yellow-and-white checked dress a chance to swirl out, the brown lace flaring; then she was gone.

Kerri stared after her for a moment, then sighed and finished dressing. The dress fit perfectly, and when she stood in front of the mirror, she was surprised to see that she looked almost pretty. If Jamie could see her now, she thought, then forced her mind away from such thoughts.

"Kerri, are you about ready?" Bob called from beyond her room door.

"Be right out," Kerri replied, dabbing on some light lipstick and giving her hair a final pat. She owed it to her mother and to Bob to try being the kind of daughter everyone would expect to meet.

The long shadows of the pines stretched across the parking area and the rough grass of the lawn to where the flagstones had been set in the ground to form a large, level terrace. The cooking pit was located at the outer edge, and Bob was already there, supervising as Mrs. O'Roarke, the cook, worked over the meat that was already filling the air with wonderful smells. Kerri followed her mother across the flagstones to where the long table had been set up.

"Just put the beans on the hot tray," her mother instructed, setting down a huge bowl of potato salad, then moving on to inspect the contents of several other dishes.

"I'm starving," Kerri wailed. "It all smells wonderful."

"Nobody does a barbecue like Mrs. O'Roarke," a voice said from behind her.

Kerri turned so quickly her foot slipped on the flagstones. She found herself almost in Derrick Peterson's arms. "Take it easy, Kerri," he said, catching her arms to steady her. "Break a leg out here and they shoot you."

"Derrick," a girl wailed. She was taller than Kerri's five-one, very slim, with a thick mane of dark brown hair that blew lightly in the breeze off the lake. "Hi, Kerri. I'm LuAnn," she introduced herself. "Welcome to Whitefish."

"Thanks," Kerri answered, feeling slightly awkward facing the two teenagers. "I'm glad to meet you. Mom's been telling me about both of you."

"Don't believe a word of it," Derrick said. "We are quiet, obedient, almost invisible employees of this resort."

"If you believe that, you'll believe anything," Bob said, joining them. "They are terrific employees, but not quiet or obedient."

Derrick chuckled. "Where is everybody?" he asked.

"On their way," Bob answered.

"Good. I'm starving," LuAnn contributed.

"You're always starving," Bob told her unsympa-

thetically; then he turned to Kerri. "To look at that
child, you'd think LuAnn's parents never fed her, but
I swear I've seen her eat more than three football
players."

LuAnn blushed and giggled, seeming not the slight-
est bit embarrassed. "I'm just a growing girl," she
answered.

"If you had any decency, you'd get fat," Bob
teased. "Introduce my girl around, will you, when the
rest of the kids get here? I'm going to open some wine
for your parents."

Her stepfather left them, returning to the table
where two more adults were talking to her mother and
Mrs. O'Roarke. Kerri watched Bob till he joined
them, then turned back to Derrick and LuAnn. The
silence stretched out between them.

"So, how do you like the place?" Derrick asked at
last.

"It's beautiful," Kerri replied. "Of course, I
haven't seen anything but the lodge and the lakeshore."

"Did you pick a horse yet?" LuAnn asked.

Kerri nodded. "Sky Writer."

"What?" The girl's blue eyes met Kerri's hazel
ones. "Didn't Mr. Harriman tell you about her?"

"She's beautiful and she acts really gentle," Kerri
protested.

"She's also totally undependable," LuAnn warned.
"She shies, and if she gets you out of position, she'll
buck you off. Then she'll leave you."

"How well do you ride, Kerri?" Derrick asked.

"I've been riding since I was a little kid," Kerri
said.

"Do you have your own horse?" LuAnn asked.

"Well, no, not in Spokane," Kerri admitted. "But I could ride any horse at the riding stable, and some of them were pretty lively."

"Sky Writer is more than lively," Derrick stated. "She's tricky. I don't know what's wrong with her, but she's not the horse for you, Kerri. In fact, I doubt that she's a fit mount for anyone."

Kerri tossed back her auburn hair. "Well, Bob promised me that I could have any horse I wanted, and I want Sky Writer. She likes me."

"Hey, Kerri, she's great on the ground," LuAnn broke in. "I mean, she is like a tall dog. She used to follow me all over when I was working with the other horses, but once you start riding her, she changes."

Kerri opened her mouth to tell them that she'd take her chances, but before she could say anything, two cars emerged from the shadows under the pines that guarded the road. Both the Petersons turned away from her.

"That must be the rest of the crew," LuAnn said.

"Come on over and I'll introduce you," Derrick said, leading the way across the flagstones to where the cars were parking. LuAnn followed Kerri, so the three of them were standing at the edge of the terrace when the six young people came around the corner.

Derrick introduced her to Lucille Rogers, a tall brunette; Josie Snyder, a slightly pudgy girl; and Sandy Kline, a very pretty blonde with cool blue eyes. Three young men followed: Perry Snyder, Josie's older brother; Les Burns, a stocky, dark-haired boy; and Myron Fuller.

Kerri caught her breath in a soft gasp as Myron Fuller stepped around the corner. He was tall, over six feet, and handsome as a movie star. His blond hair looked almost white against his tanned face; his gray eyes were pale. When he looked at her, he didn't smile, but his look was like a caress. "So this is Kerri McGuire," he said.

Kerri knew that her hello was weak and a little squeaky, but she couldn't help herself. Everyone else seemed to simply fade away as she lost herself in those wonderful, penetrating eyes. All at once she was very, very glad to be in Whitefish and working at the Lakeside Resort.

"You can close your mouth now," a low voice whispered in her ear, returning Kerri to reality. She felt the red rising in her cheeks, and anger flared behind her embarrassment as she whirled to face LuAnn Peterson. However, before she could make some devastating reply, she saw the sympathy in the younger girl's face.

"He always has that effect," LuAnn continued as the rest of the young people walked away from them. "There isn't a girl in Whitefish High that isn't completely flipped over him—except maybe Sandy."

"I feel like an idiot," Kerri admitted.

"Join the club," LuAnn said without sympathy.

"He'll think I'm really gross."

"He'll just accept it as his due," LuAnn corrected. "Myron expects to be adored. As Derrick says, he's not conceited, he's convinced." She sighed. "Actually, most of the guys like him, so I guess he's not too bad. It's just that he's gorgeous."

"Hey, LuAnn, Kerri, come on, the beef is ready," Derrick called from the fire-pit area.

Kerri moved across the flagstones obediently, suddenly conscious that Myron's gray eyes were on her. She shouldn't pay any attention, she told herself.

After all, just yesterday Jamie had kissed her; and in a year he might even be going to the University of Montana so she could date him. Those magical thoughts helped to ease the impact of being near Myron Fuller, but they couldn't really ease her shyness.

3

Joining the grouping of young people didn't actually put her into their circle. Sandy, whose white ruffled blouse and full red skirt made the most of a terrific figure, was talking to Perry and Myron while Les and Derrick talked about horses and Lucille stared at Myron. Only Josie smiled at Kerri.

"So, how do you like it?" she asked.

"I'd love to come here on vacation," Kerri admitted. "I think I'm going to be jealous of the guests."

"No, you won't," Derrick corrected her, turning from his conversation with Les. "You'll soon find out that we have a lot more fun than they do. Besides, they have to leave after a week or two; we don't."

"That's what everyone says," Josie agreed. "Perry put in his application for a second year right after Labor Day last year, so he was sure that he could come back."

"And you decided to keep it in the family," Kerri observed, feeling a twinge of envy. She'd always wished she had a brother or sister. "That's neat."

"Also essential," Josie said. "With two of us in college this fall, the folks aren't going to be able to manage anything more than tuition and housing. I'm working for my college wardrobe and all the other extras."

"Don't talk about working," Bob interrupted. "Tell her about the rides and the picnics, the parties on the lake, the trips into the hills. Make it sound like a vacation. She'll find out that I'm a slave driver later."

"You mean when she sees the big whip you carry, Mr. Harriman?" Derrick asked with a chuckle.

"Right." Bob nodded. "Now come on, don't be shy. Get up there and fill your plates. We got enough food for an army, and if I remember rightly from last year's crew, that should just about be enough."

General laughter eased them to the table where Mrs. O'Roarke and Kerri's mother were waiting to help dish up the food. Kerri moved into the line slowly, timing her arrival to put her beside Myron.

"Is this your first season of working at the resort?" she asked, hoping that he wouldn't notice how her hands were shaking as she ladled food onto her plate.

"Sure is," he said. "I'll be learning the ropes just like you."

His eyes stopped her breathing for several seconds; she added a second spoonful of baked beans without even realizing that she'd put the first one on. "I guess we'll have to depend on Derrick and Perry for instruction," she managed, stopping herself just in time before she added a third spoon of the beans.

"You do ride, don't you?" Myron asked.

"Sure," Kerri said. "I haven't been on a horse

much this past year, but I used to practically live at the riding stable when I was a kid." She paused, then asked, "What about you? Do you have a horse of your own?"

Myron laughed easily, piling the tender barbecued beef on his plate. "I used to have one, but I've been too busy the past couple of years, so you and I will have to do some riding in our spare time, I guess. Get back into practice before the long rides start."

"I think I need a little practice, too," Sandy observed in a silky voice. "I haven't done too much riding, either."

"Why don't we all take a short ride tomorrow?" Derrick suggested, spoiling the picture Kerri had been building in her mind. "Give us a chance to try some of the horses on the easier trails and get you softies into condition."

"If I wasn't going off to play college ball, I'd show you who was a softie on the football field, Peterson," Myron said.

Derrick grinned at him. "I wouldn't call you a softie out there," he admitted.

"I think a ride sounds like fun," Josie put in, her green eyes bright. "I don't really need the conditioning, but I'd love to see the trails you use for the guests."

"Tomorrow about ten?" Derrick looked around, then turned to Bob. "Okay, Mr. Harriman?"

"You're the wrangler," Bob told him. "If you want to practice on your friends, it's all right with me."

Everyone laughed and they moved slowly toward the smaller tables. Kerri was so confused, she missed her chance to sit with Myron and found herself instead at the table with Derrick, LuAnn and Josie Snyder.

The conversation was brisk and friendly, but Kerri

couldn't help feeling left out as they talked about people and parties and activities that had no meaning for her. Even LuAnn, who hadn't said a word while they were in line at the table, responded to Josie's easy giggles and her brother's teasing. LuAnn was, Kerri realized, even more shy than she was.

"Will you be working here, LuAnn?" Kerri asked when there was a break in the conversation.

"Sort of unofficially," LuAnn answered. "I help with the rides and do baby-sitting for guests who need someone to take care of their children while they're here."

"She takes out the pony riders," Derrick supplied. "Those are the little kids who aren't old enough or interested enough to go on the rides with the adults. Mr. Harriman has a couple of ponies that are gentle enough to trust with a baby, and LuAnn is in charge of them."

"Sounds like quite a job," Kerri observed, realizing that it was true.

"It's fun," LuAnn said.

"For you maybe," Josie commented, rolling her eyes and shaking her head. "I'd much rather ride with the big kids."

LuAnn giggled. "Like Les?" she teased.

"Or Myron?" Derrick added.

"I think that is hopeless," Josie replied. "Everybody knows that Sandy only applied here so she could keep an eye on him." She looked down at her rather ample shape. "There's no way I can compete with her."

"Maybe she'll get so sore after tomorrow's ride she'll decide she doesn't want the job," LuAnn suggested. "We could put her on Poncho. He's got the roughest trot of any horse I've ever ridden."

Derrick shook his head. "I think I should go sit at the other table," he said. "You girls are too wicked for me."

"You just want to go flirt with Sandy," LuAnn teased.

"Not really," Derrick said, and Kerri felt his eyes on her face. "Actually, I think I'd rather stay here and talk to Kerri, if she's still willing to talk to us, the way we've been carrying on."

The warmth of his voice made Kerri smile, and in a moment she found herself answering questions about her life in Spokane. She felt a pang of homesickness as she described the things she'd done, the parties, the clubs and activities that had filled her days and evenings.

"But that's all over now," she ended, abruptly deciding that she didn't want to talk about it anymore. "What do you do here?"

"Well, there's not much beyond the lake and the horses in the summer," Derrick answered. "We have gymkhanas and rodeos and horse shows. There's the county fair in the fall, and the Ridge Riders have a couple of special things scheduled every month."

"What is the Ridge Riders?" Kerri asked.

"The riding club," LuAnn answered. "You belong. Or, anyway, Mr. Harriman does, so you're automatically a member, you and your mom."

"Mom doesn't ride," Kerri protested.

"Well, she's been trying," Derrick told her with a grin. "She's not doing too badly, either."

Kerri giggled. "That I have to see. Mom always said she was scared to death of horses."

"On a dude ranch?" Josie laughed.

"Well, I suppose if Bob wanted her to learn—"

Kerri began, then was interrupted by the sudden blaring of music from a portable radio.

"Sounds like your stepfather is ready to dance," Derrick said, holding out his hand to Kerri. "Want to join them?"

For a moment she hesitated, not wanting to be one of the first couples on the flagstone floor; afraid of making a fool of herself by not being able to follow Derrick's lead or by stumbling over her own feet. But the challenge in his dark eyes was too insistent. "I'd like that," she murmured, getting up.

Much to her relief, not only her family, but the Petersons and Myron and Sandy were also dancing, so she felt a little less conspicuous. Still, it seemed strange to be dancing to something as old-fashioned as a waltz, and she couldn't help feeling a little shy with Derrick's hard-muscled arm around her.

"Don't let the music fool you," Derrick whispered. "As soon as the old folks go inside for the evening, we'll get some rock."

Kerri giggled. "I was afraid to ask," she confided.

"We're not that deep in the country," he chided. "We may not have all the newest steps, but we get by; and when it comes to country and western . . ." He let it trail off, then asked, "Do you square-dance?"

Kerri shook her head. "I've seen it done, but no one in our crowd was into it."

"Maybe this winter you'll change your mind. There's a neat square dance club at school and they're always looking for couples to join. It's a nice way to make friends."

"Sounds great," Kerri said, looking up at him through her thick, red-brown lashes. What did he mean? she wondered. Was he really thinking of her as a part of a couple? Or was it just an offhand remark that he'd forget as soon as he started dancing with someone else?

"I really appreciate the way you talked to LuAnn this evening," Derrick went on.

"What do you mean?" Kerri asked, startled by the change of subject.

He grinned and looked uncomfortable. "Well, she's usually pretty shy at anything like this. She's younger than everybody and she isn't dating or anything, so . . . You know what I mean."

Kerri nodded, realizing that up until just the past three months, those words would have pretty well described both her and Donna. "She's nice," she observed, aware that he expected something from her.

"She's horse-crazy," Derrick corrected her. "The only time she really comes alive is when there are horses around. I swear she'll never date a boy till she finds one with four legs and a whinny."

Kerri giggled as Derrick whirled her across the terrace. "I'm going to have to depend on her for some advice," she told Derrick after she caught her breath. "I really don't know much about horses except how to ride them."

"Just ask your friendly ranch wrangler anything you want to know," he drawled as the music ended. "I taught LuAnn everything she knows."

Kerri thought of the dainty pinto mare and the strange way everyone seemed to dislike her. "Thanks. I just might," she said as they returned to the table where Bob was waiting.

"Hate to steal her away from you, Derrick," he said, "but I've got to get my dances while the music is in my speed."

Derrick laughed, and Kerri found herself being swung back out onto the dance floor by her stepfather. "Having a good time, Kerri?" he asked.

Kerri nodded. "This is a nice party," she told him. "Thank you for doing it."

"You know how much it means to your mother and me to have you here, Kerri. We want you to be happy and to learn to love this place as much as we do." His dark eyes were level in his weathered cowboy face.

"I want to love it too," Kerri assured him.

"Anytime you want to invite some of your friends from Spokane to come over, you just set it up with your mother. She's in charge of reservations." Bob grinned down at her. "We don't want you to get lonesome while you're making new friends here."

"Thanks, Bob, that would be great," Kerri said. "My best friend, Donna . . . well, I sort of promised her that she could come over as soon as I was settled."

"Whenever she can get away." He swung her out lightly, setting her skirts to whirling, then danced her back toward the table just as the music ended.

"How about the next one, Kerri?" The voice was deep; and when Kerri turned, her heart leaped as she met Myron's gaze.

The music was faster, and Kerri felt a twinge of uncertainty as Myron took her hand. However, she had no opportunity for doubt as he led her. His expertise made her look far better than she was, and the music seemed to actually grip her feet and direct them. She was laughing when the flare of a flashbulb told her that her mother had taken out her camera and was busy recording the party.

" 'Candid Camera' strikes," she said with a giggle. "My mother, the mad photographer."

"I heard that she's going to try to do a brochure for

the resort," Myron told her, grinning in a way that made her pulses race. "Think she's going to make us famous?"

"Why not?" Kerri asked, thinking that any brochure showing Myron on the cover would attract a lot of girls to the resort. She sobered slightly. "Mom used to do advertising work with her photography before my dad was killed," she told Myron. "Only it didn't pay regularly, so she had to give it up and go back into bookkeeping. She'll do a terrific brochure."

"Anytime she wants to take pictures . . ." Myron murmured, twirling her lightly and easily.

"Time to light the lanterns," Bob announced once the music stopped. Kerri sank down at the table with a sigh, watching as the men lit the four lanterns, one at each corner of the terrace. They made small pools of light, but did little to penetrate the darkness that spread out on all sides.

Kerri looked out and shivered, feeling the cool breeze that came off the lake. It was nothing like home, she realized suddenly. At home there were streetlights and the friendly glow from neighbors' windows; but here there was nothing but the darkness of the lake and the darkness of the hills.

"What's wrong?" LuAnn asked.

"It just seems so lonely out here," Kerri explained. "I didn't realize it till it got dark."

"You can see a couple of the resorts along the lakeshore," LuAnn said, leaning forward. "Only I guess they aren't open yet, either. In a couple of weeks there'll be more lights around there. Once the season starts. Winter is when it gets kind of lonesome."

"For you?" Kerri was surprised.

"Oh, for—" LuAnn stopped. Kerri looked up to see Perry Snyder standing behind her.

"Dance, Kerri?" he asked.

The evening picked up as the adults adjourned to the house and Myron changed the radio to a rock station. Kerri danced till she was breathless and dizzy from the pace and from the nearness of Myron Fuller, who seemed to be splitting his time almost evenly between her and Sandy Kline.

She was sorry when Bob came back out bearing a huge cake and a large, old-fashioned ice-cream freezer. "Time for dessert," he said. "At least, I assume you've worked off dinner by now."

"Dessert is his way of telling us it's time to go home," Derrick whispered to Kerri. "He uses it all summer when he wants to get the guests inside so he can go to bed."

Kerri laughed. "I can see where I've got a lot to learn about running a resort," she observed. "That's sneaky."

"I hate to see the evening end this time," Derrick observed, then blushed. "It's more fun now you're here," he added.

"I've had a wonderful time," Kerri agreed, touched by his openness, which seemed so different from the boys she'd been around in Spokane. No one there had ever said anything like that to her, not even Jamie on that last afternoon.

Thinking of Jamie brought a wave of depression, and she was glad that everyone else was distracted by the cutting of the cake and the dishing up of the wonderful homemade ice cream. Why had Jamie chosen to wait till it was too late to notice her? she asked herself bitterly. Why hadn't he asked her out while school was still in session and they had a chance?

"Tired, honey?" her mother asked, breaking into her thoughts.

"I guess so," Kerri admitted. "It's been a long day."

"We did start kind of early," her mother agreed, stretching and yawning, "but it sure is good to be home."

They all pulled chairs up to the long redwood serving table to eat their cake and ice cream and to drink mugs of coffee, tea or hot chocolate. "Enjoy," Bob advised from the head of the table. "This will be our last private party till after we close in September."

"Don't remind me," Mrs. O'Roarke groaned. "Makes my feet hurt just thinking about the mob that will be descending in a couple of days."

"Hey, don't scare off the crew," Bob warned her.

"It'll take more than sore feet to scare me off," Myron commented, slanting a glance in Kerri's direction.

"You'll get more than sore feet the first time you take a ride up to High Meadows," Perry told him amid general laughter.

"We'll all start toughening up tomorrow," Les reminded them.

"Ten o'clock," Derrick agreed; then added, "Wear your bathing suits under your jeans if you want to. There's still a pond back in the hills, and the water is a lot warmer there this time of year than it is in the lake."

"How about a lunch?" Kerri's mother asked.

"Oh, we can all bring sandwiches," Derrick said.

"I'll fix a lunch," Mrs. O'Roarke overruled him. "There's enough food left from tonight to fix up something."

Derrick grinned at the woman. "When Mrs. O'Roarke fixes up something, you'd better be prepared to use a packhorse."

Mrs. O'Roarke laughed with the rest of them, and Kerri leaned back in her chair, staring up at the black velvet of the sky, savoring the strange feeling of family that seemed to spread over the entire group. Would it always be like this? she wondered. Or would the days ahead change everything? Would working together make them all closer, or would they be too busy for this feeling of fun?

All too soon the evening ended, and Kerri stood on the edge of the terrace waving good-bye to everyone as they got into their cars and disappeared into the trees. She felt her mother's arm around her shoulders as they went inside; then she was alone in her room, so tired and sleepy she barely had the strength to strip off her dress, pull on pajamas and collapse into bed. She was asleep before she could even think about the new world she had entered.

The sunlight woke her, streaming across her pillow. Kerri sat up and looked around, not sure where she was for a moment; then the whole wonderful evening filled her mind and she sank back against her pillow, smiling.

Wait'll I write Donna, she thought smugly, picturing how she'd describe both Myron and Derrick and, of course, the resort and the rest of the staff. Donna would be dying to visit, she was sure—and, naturally, she'd tell Jamie all about everything Kerri wrote.

Would he be jealous? Kerri wondered. It would be nice if he was just a little bit, since he'd waited till the very last day to even notice her. She tried to picture Jamie coming to the resort. He'd love it, of course, but she'd be so busy with everything, she wouldn't really have a lot of time to spend with him.

A sound forced her mind back from the daydream, and she looked up as her mother opened the door a crack and peeked in, then entered. "So you're awake," she said. "I wanted to let you sleep as long as you could. Today is going to be busy for you."

"How about you?" Kerri asked. "Are you going on the ride with us? Derrick says you're learning to ride."

Her mother winced. "I'm not good enough for any real rides yet," she admitted, "but I'm not afraid of horses anymore, anyway. Bob says by next year he'll be making me wrangler, but I think he's joking."

"You really love it, don't you?" Kerri couldn't keep the envy out of her voice.

"I think you will too," her mother said. "You had fun last night, didn't you?"

"It was a neat party."

"Would you like prints of the pictures I took to send to Donna when you write?"

"Could I?"

"Sure. I'm going to develop the film this afternoon. Bob and I set up a darkroom in the ranch house, and I'm anxious to see what I've got. If any of them are good enough, I'll use them in the promotional brochure."

"Be sure and pick one with Myron in it," Kerri advised her. "He'll bring you dozens of young girls."

"He's certainly a looker," her mother agreed.

"Dreamy." Kerri enjoyed talking to her mother so openly. "LuAnn says all the girls in high school were crazy about him."

"Well, he certainly seemed impressed with you."

Kerri sighed. "He was probably just trying to make Sandy jealous," she admitted wryly.

"I don't know. You have to remember you're the new girl in town, Kerri." Her mother's usually laughing eyes became serious. "There's no reason why he wouldn't find you very attractive. You've become a pretty young lady the past few months. Jamie Palmer noticed it, so why shouldn't the young men here?"

"Do you really think—" Kerri began, daring to dream just a little.

"I think you should be careful," her mother said. "Myron is a couple of years older than you and out of school, so it might not be a good idea to get too involved with him. Remember, he'll be leaving in the fall."

"That leaves three whole months," Kerri reminded her.

"Derrick seemed pretty attentive too," her mother persisted. "He's a very nice boy."

"LuAnn is nice too," Kerri added. "Derrick says she's very shy."

"Bob was telling me about that. He seemed pleased at the way you had her talking. I really think he's been like an uncle to those two kids, probably because he never had any of his own to fuss about till now."

Their eyes met, and Kerri winced away, unable to do what she knew her mother wanted her to. It was much too soon for Bob to begin taking her father's place. She felt guilty even considering such a thing.

"Breakfast is ready," her mother told her, getting up and heading for the door. "Why don't you put on a robe and come out and eat before you get dressed?"

"I didn't think I'd ever be hungry after last night," Kerri said, getting up, "but somehow . . ."

Her mother laughed. "I know what you mean. If there wasn't so much work to be done, I know I'd have gained twenty pounds already."

After breakfast there was a tour of the lodge's guest rooms—all of which were on the second floor—and then a peek into two of the cabins, which Kerri found much more inviting. "If I was coming here, I'd want to be in a cabin," she confided. "The rooms are okay, but they're just like any hotel. The cabins look like something out of a movie."

"They have their disadvantages," her mother said. "If it rains, you have a long, wet walk to all your meals."

"Everyone eats in the dining room?" Kerri asked, thinking of the neatly arranged tables and chairs and the shiny wood floor.

"Unless we have a cookout; then it's handled just the way the barbecue was last night—I guess." Her mother's smile became a little shaky. "I've never been here for the season either, you know."

"Gee, I hope we don't put Bob out of business," Kerri teased.

"Thanks a lot," her mother answered, then pointed across the grass toward the corrals. "Look, there's Derrick and LuAnn now. Why don't you go down and give them a hand with saddling up? And you'll have to pick your own horse too, won't you? Bob said you looked at them yesterday."

"I'm going to ride Sky Writer," Kerri said. "And yes, I think I should go down and help them saddle the horses. Maybe they can tell me more about her."

"See you later then."

4

Kerri slowed as she neared the corrals, some of her resolve fading as she remembered how both Derrick and LuAnn had reacted to her interest in the pinto mare. She watched silently as the brother and sister moved about the corrals catching horses and bringing them out to tie them to the rails. Soon there were seven horses standing there, not counting the two Derrick and LuAnn had ridden over, and none of them was Sky Writer.

"What are you doing?" Kerri asked, moving up to the corral fence.

"Getting the horses for the ride," Derrick answered, giving her an odd stare. "Don't tell me you forgot already?"

"Where's my horse?" Kerri inquired, ignoring his teasing tone.

"I thought you'd probably like Cinder," Derrick

said, reaching out to rub the head of a compact black gelding. "He's got plenty of life, but he's a good trail horse and—"

"I want Sky Writer," Kerri interrupted. "I told you that last night."

"Come on, Kerri, we told you she's not a good horse for you."

"I think she is," Kerri said as the black-and-white nose came over the rail to sniff at her arm. "See, she likes me. She'll be fun to ride."

"She's nothing but trouble," Derrick protested. "I really don't think—"

"Bob said I could have any horse I want," Kerri reminded him, "and I want Sky Writer. She'll be fine, you'll see." She stroked the sleek black-and-white neck, smoothing the long mane all over on one side.

Derrick opened his mouth as though he'd like to protest further, then closed it and untied the gelding, leading him back into the corral. Then he caught the pinto and brought her out. "Here you go," he said, handing Kerri the leadrope. "Take her into the stable and we'll start saddling and bridling."

Kerri took the rope; she felt better when the mare's pretty head came to press against her shoulder as they walked across the rough grass to the open stable door. As they walked inside, LuAnn came out of the tack room, her arms full of bridles. She opened her mouth to say something, but her brother must have signaled her not to, because after a moment she just said "Hi" and handed Kerri a bridle.

By the time she'd finished bridling and saddling the mare and one of the other horses, Kerri was caught between apprehension and defiance. Sky Writer was gentle and friendly to work with, much more so than any of the horses she'd known at the stable; but both Derrick and LuAnn had seemed so sure that she would cause trouble, Kerri couldn't completely relax.

Finally, as they secured the now-saddled horses to the corral rail to wait for the arrival of the rest of the staff, Kerri moved over to stand beside LuAnn. "Ah . . . what really happened with Sky Writer, LuAnn?" she asked. "I mean, Derrick said that you rode her a lot last year."

LuAnn's thin features took on a grim look. "I don't know," she said at last, reaching out a hand to stroke the friendly mare almost reluctantly. "I guess that's why I'm so down on her. I really thought she was the best mare in the string, maybe the best horse on the place."

"So what happened?" Kerri watched the girl's face.

LuAnn shook her head. "She's kind of spooky, you know. She shies at things; but I was used to that. We just never let any guests ride her for that reason."

Kerri nodded. "I used to ride a big bay gelding at the stable who shied. The head man there said that it might be his eyes. Horses see differently than people do because of the way their eyes are placed on the sides of their heads. He seemed to think old Bugler might have something wrong with one eye that made him see things in scary ways."

LuAnn considered, then shook her head. "That's not it with Sky Writer," she said. "She's just kind of high-strung. You can ride her past a cement mixer, but if a squirrel runs by her on the trail, she comes apart."

"Is that why you don't like her?" Kerri asked, sensing that there was much more.

LuAnn sighed. "Heck, no. She can't help that."

"So what happened?"

LuAnn moved away from Sky Writer, turning her back to the mare as though she didn't even want to look at her. "It was on a ride late last year. The only one we took to Bear Meadows." She paused, then explained. "Bear Meadows is pretty far up in the hills, so we only take the guests up if we happen to have a group of fairly experienced riders."

LuAnn stopped for several minutes, seeming to concentrate on smoothing several forelocks over the browbands of bridles, then she continued. "Sky Writer started out all right, but she got really weird when we headed up into the hills. She was shying at shadows and acting like she'd never been in the woods before."

She stopped again, and after several minutes Kerri finally asked, "So what happened?"

"Well, she was rotten all the way to the meadows, so I decided to ride drag going back so she wouldn't upset any of the guest horses. I figured that she'd be tired enough to settle down, but I was wrong."

"What do you mean?"

"I held her back when the group started out, and she really got strange. Then when we started down the trail, she just came apart. She shied all over the place, stumbled on the rocks and . . . and then she bucked me off and left me. She tore down the mountain through the trees like a deer, and as far as I know, she didn't stop till she got to the corral."

"Good grief." Kerri swallowed hard. "What happened to you?"

"Well, Sky Writer missed the group of riders completely. They didn't even see her in the trees, so no one missed me till they were clear down to the bottom of the trail and out into the open. Luckily, there were four of the staff with the group, so Derrick rode back up the trail and found me."

"You weren't hurt?"

LuAnn grinned at her. "One of the first things you learn when you ride is how to fall off. I got a couple of bruises and a large hole in my pride." She shook her head. "I've been thrown plenty, but Sky Writer is the first horse that's ever left me like that. Most of them will run off a little bit, but she was just anxious to get rid of me and get out of there. I don't think anything would have stopped her."

Kerri shook her head, looking back at the mare. "I can't imagine her doing something like that," she said. "She seems so gentle and sweet."

"That's the worst part," LuAnn agreed. "You're better off with a rotten horse, if it's consistently rotten. You can't really ever trust Sky Writer, because you'll never know when she's going to have one of those weird fits and leave you along the trail."

"Has anyone ridden her since?" Kerri asked.

"Sure." LuAnn sighed. "I was determined to find out what was wrong with her, so I rode her every chance I got. Mr. Harriman even let me take her back to our ranch with me and use her there."

"So what happened?"

"Nothing." LuAnn shrugged. "That's what finally made me give up. She was just the same as she'd been before. It was like it never happened."

"Maybe there was something up on that trail that really scared her, LuAnn," Kerri suggested. "Something that you didn't see."

LuAnn shook her head. "I was there a long time after she left me, and there wasn't anything, Kerri. Besides, she was acting up before we stopped there.

That was why I held her back to ride drag on the way down. You just can't ever trust her."

"Is that why everyone wants to get rid of her?"

"No one *wants* to get rid of her," LuAnn corrected, a touch of anger in her voice. "It's just that no one wants a four-legged time bomb around a bunch of inexperienced riders. What if one of the guests had been riding her that afternoon? They could have been seriously hurt or the other horses could have been spooked into a full-scale disaster."

"But if she was my very own horse, no one else would be riding her," Kerri protested.

LuAnn shrugged. "So ride her. Maybe she'll be fine for you, who knows? Maybe it was a one-time thing; but, Kerri, don't ever trust her. There is something wrong with that mare, and I don't want you to get hurt finding it out."

Kerri nodded, her feelings about the ride ahead mixed now that she'd heard the full story. Though she didn't want to, she was forced to believe LuAnn. The girl had cared a great deal about Sky Writer and she obviously knew a lot about horses.

Should she change horses now? she asked herself. She was sure that no one would laugh at her or call her coward. A soft muzzle nuzzled at her arm, and she turned to see that Sky Writer was trying to get her attention.

"Here come the rest of them," Derrick called from the other corral, where he'd been checking the feet of a big bay.

Kerri looked toward the opening in the forest and made her decision. "I guess it's you and me, Sky Writer," she told the mare. "Maybe we can prove everybody else wrong."

* * *

In spite of Kerri's initial fears, the ride proved to be fun. Sky Writer was spirited, dancing and eager when they set off in a ragged line to follow Derrick on his tall Appaloosa gelding. Kerri was nervous, because of Sky Writer and because she was riding with the staff she would be sharing the summer with. However, the beauty of the lake and woods quickly eased the worst of her doubts.

"You are a good rider," Myron said, guiding his horse alongside the dainty mare. "And you look terrific on the horse."

"Thank you," Kerri answered, aware that she was blushing at the compliment and hating herself for it. "How are you doing?"

"I may never walk again, but I guess it'll be worth it." He grinned lazily. "Perry has done nothing but talk about the cute girls who come here on vacation, so I'll just have to toughen up so I can go on the moonlight rides."

"Moonlight rides?" Kerri was surprised.

"About one a week," Perry answered from just ahead of them. "We ride along the ridge trail and then have a steak fry; later we ride back in the moonlight. The guests love it."

"It does sound like fun," Kerri murmured. "In fact, everything does."

"Oh, we're going to have a terrific summer, Kerri, that I guarantee." Myron leaned across to give her shoulder a promising squeeze that set her pulses racing and drove all thoughts about Sky Writer from her mind.

Perry went on entertaining them with stories of last summer's adventures, some of which Kerri suspected were more than a little exaggerated. Still, he was a gifted storyteller, and she laughed so hard she was tired by the time Derrick halted the group on the edge of a small meadow.

"Here we are," he announced. "Unsaddle your horses and turn them loose with their reins dragging, then we can take a quick dip before we eat."

Kerri looked across the high grass to where a small pool nestled, half shaded by the towering pines that edged the meadow. Since the sun had been bright and hot on the ride up, the sparkle of the water was very inviting.

Though she was a little shy as she unbuttoned her shirt and unzipped her Levi's, the others were less inhibited, shouting and laughing as they stripped off their outerwear to reveal the bathing suits they wore underneath. Only LuAnn appeared to share her shyness, and as a result, they were the last two to jump into the still, cool water.

They splashed about, the boys diving beneath the crystal waters to grab the girls' ankles to dunk them. Lucille, her dark hair streaming, produced a bright red ball that bobbed on the water and set up a sort of tag game that had no real rules but required a great deal of splashing, diving and laughing.

By the time they emerged, dripping and exhausted, Kerri felt as at home with the group as she had with her friends in Spokane. She untied her towel from behind her saddle and spread it on the grass, collapsing in the sun with a moan.

She'd lain there only a moment when the end of a towel snapped at her thigh. "None of that now," Derrick ordered. "Time to practice being staff members. The hampers are over there."

Kerri sat up, groaning. "I thought you said Bob was the slave driver," she protested.

"I'm his stand-in," Derrick told her with a grin. "Go on, girls, go set out the lunch."

"What are you guys going to do?" Sandy asked.

"Rest," was the universal answer.

Sandy nodded, then led the way around the pond to where Derrick had placed the two large hampers in the shade. "Are we going to take that?" she asked as soon as they were out of earshot.

"What can we do?" Josie asked, her eyes sparkling as she tugged at her bright orange suit.

"Well, we could eat all the food before we call them," Lucille suggested, opening the first hamper.

"Wrong!" Sandy said, opening the other. "We may be taking some of this back. That Mrs. O'Roarke must think we brought a bunch of guests with us."

"We could put their food in one hamper and toss it into the pond," Josie suggested. "I think—"

"I think you could use some help," said a deep voice from directly behind them. "There seems to be too much talk over here and not enough action."

Kerri whirled and found herself looking up into Myron's gray eyes. He was grinning, but there was a wickedness about his eyes that told her he'd overheard most of what was said. "Hungry?" she asked.

"Starved," he said, draping a casual arm around her shoulders as he moved up to peer into the hampers. "What do we have?"

The food seemed to melt under their attack, and in spite of what Sandy had said, there was little left by the time they all collapsed on their towels. Kerri tried to relax, but she was terribly conscious that Myron had spread his towel beside hers.

"Having a good time, Kerri?" Derrick asked from the other side.

"Fantastic," she murmured, not even opening her eyes. "I just wish that today would never end."

"Don't we all," Myron agreed. "But after tomorrow we'll all be employed, and no more lying around in the sun."

"Day after tomorrow the guests start to arrive, and after that . . . it's fun, but you sure don't have a lot of time to think about it," Perry supplied from the other side of the hampers.

"If a lazybones like you survived it, it'll be a cinch for the rest of us," Josie teased her brother.

Kerri smiled, but inside she wasn't truly sure, not about anything. What lay ahead looked very frightening, and even though she liked the group that would be going through these days with her . . .

She shivered in spite of the warm sun and longed for the day when Donna would be coming to visit.

The next day passed in a flurry of preparations as both Kerri and her mother were instructed in the basics of preparing a resort for the arrival of the first guests of the season. Bob supervised with benign laughter, correcting their errors before they finished making them.

By evening, Kerri collapsed onto one of the comfortable leather couches in the lobby, too tired to even make her way to her room. "Is it always like this?" she groaned at Bob.

His smile was innocent. "No, things will be getting busy tomorrow when the guests roll in."

"Oh Bob, don't say things like that," her mother wailed from across the room. "You'll have us both getting on the morning train for Washington."

"Oh, no, you don't," he answered. "We're all in this together and it's going to be fun, you'll see."

"We can wait," Kerri told him.

"You just need something to eat," Bob suggested. "Come on. Mrs. O'Roarke left dinner in the oven; and after dinner we'll make a couple of phone calls, all right?"

"Phone calls?" Kerri and her mother both asked at the same time.

"Well, now, I thought you just might like to call your mother, Alice, to see how things are going in her move to that new apartment. And, Kerri, I want you to call your girl friend and ask her when she's going to be able to come out here for a visit."

"You mean it?" Kerri asked, reviving at the thought.

"Of course I do," Bob assured them both. "Things will get pretty busy starting tomorrow and you won't have much time in the evenings, so we'd better use what time we have."

"You make it sound like a full-time job," her mother murmured.

"You have to be available from the time the first guest gets up till the last guest goes to bed," Bob answered. "And that can make for a long, interesting day."

Kerri waited impatiently through the phone call to her grandmother, waiting her turn to tell about the party and the ride she'd been on. Afterward, she dialed Donna's number with shaky fingers, aching to talk to her but not sure what to say.

As it turned out, she needn't have worried, for Donna was full of gossip. Kerri had little time to do more than give her the highlights. "I was just writing you a letter," Donna began. "I had to tell you about Jamie."

"What about him?" Kerri asked, her stomach knotting with remembered feelings.

"He's going steady! Can you believe that? It seems that he and Connie Fisher went out the evening after your farewell party, and the next day she had his class ring. Isn't that the wildest thing? I mean, when he offered to take you home, I thought sure that—" Donna stopped. "You two weren't getting friendly or anything, were you?" she asked after a moment.

Kerri swallowed hard, fighting a wail of pain. "How could we when I was leaving town?" she asked, glad that her mother and Bob had left her alone with the phone, glad they couldn't see her face. She only hoped that Donna wouldn't hear the hurt in her voice.

"Anyway, I guess they are the hottest duo in town," Donna continued. "So how are things going with you?"

"Terrific," Kerri managed. "Just wait till you see the pictures I'm going to send you. I told you about the big party my stepfather had last night. Well, there is this absolute dreamboat that is going to be working here and I think he likes me."

"Really? What is he like?"

"Over six foot, blond, with the sexiest gray eyes you ever saw. And, Donna, he's eighteen and going to college on a football scholarship."

Donna's moan of envy was salve for the wound to her pride. "You're going to be working with him?" she asked after a moment.

"All summer long," Kerri confirmed. "Wait till you see the pictures."

"I'll be sure and show them to Jamie," Donna told her.

"What I called about was to see when you think

you'll want to come and visit," Kerri went on, changing the subject. "Bob says you're welcome anytime."

"When will you have the most free time?" Donna asked.

Kerri leaned over the bookings list that her mother had been working on earlier. "The last week of June and the first week in August are the lightest so far," she said. "Of course, we keep taking reservations all the time, and Bob says the place runs at capacity most of the time. So it really doesn't matter. When would be best for you?"

"I don't think I can wait till August," Donna answered. "How about the last week in June? I'll have to check it out with my parents when they get home, but I don't think they'll care. Dad doesn't get his vacation till sometime later in the summer and I don't think they've even decided what they're going to do."

"Maybe you could convince them that they'd like a vacation at Lakeside Resort," Kerri teased.

"Danny would love it," Donna agreed. "He's going to be green when I tell him everything you get to do."

"I'd say bring him along in June, but I don't know where we'd put him. There are just two bedrooms in the owner's quarters," Kerri said. Donna's younger brother was the least pesky ten-year-old she'd met and they'd often included him when they went riding in Spokane.

"I'll get him to working on my folks," Donna promised. "With both of us pleading, we just might be booking the whole family into one of your cabins for a week in July or August."

There wasn't a great deal more to say, but Kerri hung up the receiver reluctantly. Just talking to Donna had revived her homesickness, and the news about Jamie . . . She cringed away from the memories of his light kiss.

She'd been a fool to think that it meant anything to him, she thought bitterly. He'd probably only offered her a ride home so he could ask her mother about a job. She blinked back tears and focused her thoughts instead on the following day. Myron would be working then and so would she, so Jamie could just go chase himself.

The next few days were the most exciting, frustrating and confusing ones that Kerri had ever spent. There were never enough hours in the day. Bob assigned her to help Josie with the maid work—for which she was grateful, since the bouncy brunette was much more fun than either Sandy or Lucille.

Once the rooms were changed and cleaned, it was time to help in the kitchen; then they had to serve lunch. As soon as lunch was cleaned up by those not assigned to the rides, there were special things to handle: riding lessons for a shy guest, watching over the swimmers on the shore, renting the rowboats that Bob kept moored to the dock. Then back to the kitchen to help with dinner, which they again served and cleaned up after.

To her disappointment, she saw little of Myron except in the dining room, where they all helped with the serving and cleaning up. Myron, after one morning of working on the grounds, proved himself a good tennis player and spent much of the day providing competition for the guests who requested him.

Perry, as the senior member of the house staff (Derrick was wrangler, and involved only in the care of the horses and the guiding and scheduling of the rides), was in charge of the boats. He checked them morning and evening, to be sure they were in good repair and that everyone who took a boat out returned with it.

By the fourth morning, Kerri felt a slight change. The confusion was gone. She moved to the kitchen as soon as she was dressed. No one had to tell her to fill the fruit-juice glasses and place them in the ice-spread cabinet with the melon slices and grapefruit halves. She toasted English muffins without burning them, set out the dishes that Mrs. O'Roarke would be filling with pancakes and eggs, sausage, bacon or ham.

As she served, she moved around the other workers without difficulty. She no longer had to watch for the tables, and she knew which of the guests were served coffee before they ordered. Breakfast was over more quickly than before, and as she stocked the small cleaning wagon for the trek to the cabins that were her and Josie's assignment, she felt secure that she hadn't forgotten anything.

"Lucky you," Josie said. "You're on the ride duty today."

"I can hardly wait," Kerri admitted, selecting the sheets and towels for the first cabin while Josie picked up the neat container that carried their cleaning supplies. "Where do we go, do you know?"

"You mean you didn't check the schedule?" Josie looked shocked. "Today is the first moonlight ride, you lucky dog."

"You're kidding." Kerri giggled. "I had no idea. I mean, when we drew lots, I just noticed the date that I drew, nothing else."

"I checked right away. I'm on the first ride to the meadow where the pond is. Guess maybe I'll get another chance to go swimming there."

"What time does the moonlight ride leave?" Kerri asked.

"About two thirty, I think." Josie's eyes sparkled. "Plenty of time for you to help with the lunch cleanup, I'm afraid."

Kerri laughed. "The funny part is, I don't even mind anymore. I sort of thought I wouldn't like this part." She tapped on the door, then when there was no answer, used her passkey, calling routinely before stepping inside. "I mean, I was never real big on cleaning and bed-making when I lived in Spokane."

Josie giggled. "Me either, but this is fun. Besides, we have the boat excursion, which should be neat. And there's the dance Saturday night."

5

Josie and Kerri worked smoothly together, changing the beds. One swept out the rooms while the other cleaned the bath and collected the garbage that had accumulated through the day.

"What happens tonight, do you know?" Kerri asked. "I mean, what about dinner?"

"We serve it out there. The guests who don't ride horseback go with us in the truck and station wagon. Perry told me all about it last year. He said that Mr. Harriman and Mrs. O'Roarke cook all the steaks, and there are potatoes and all kinds of vegetables roasted in the coals—plus salad and corn bread and ice-cold watermelon for dessert."

"Stop. You're making me hungry," Kerri complained.

"Then you get to ride back through the moonlight while the rest of the staff cleans up the mess and brings everything back down to the lodge," Josie continued.

"Wow, I really got the lucky draw, didn't I?" Kerri said, glad that it was true; that it had only been luck and not favoritism. The first morning, they had all taken turns drawing slips of paper from a hat, each one giving a simple date so that the rotation could be set up. They were free to trade dates if they liked, but the original draw had set up a schedule to work from.

"You and Perry," Josie agreed. "He has the High Falls ride. That's for all day, with a picnic by one of the prettiest falls in the area."

"I suppose by the end of the summer, everybody has been on every ride," Kerri observed as they finished the first cabin and moved on to the next. "I mean, six rides a week and seven of us drawing, we're bound to get something different every time."

"Like next week we'll have the lodge rooms to clean, and Lucille and Sandy will have the long hike to the cabins," Josie agreed. "Mr. Harriman has everything worked out pretty fairly, except for some people." She looked meaningfully toward the tennis courts where Myron was exchanging volleys with an older woman. "Of course, who could expect him to really work?" There was no malice in her tone, just a touch of wry humor.

"When it gets hot and muggy, that's going to be a whole lot more work than this," Kerri reminded her.

Josie laughed. "I just wish I had some special talent I could use," she admitted.

"Me too," Kerri agreed. "I wonder if the Warner boy who's coming tomorrow will be cute. Mom says he's a teenager, according to their reservation, but they didn't say how old."

"With our luck, he'll be thirteen and into fishing or something." They both giggled as Josie tapped on the next door.

The rest of the morning went smoothly, and once the luncheon debris had been cleared away and the dishes safely packed into the dishwasher, Kerri went out onto the terrace to catch a breath of fresh air and cool off before changing into her riding boots. They all wore Levi's and western shirts to work in, so she had little else to do in preparation for the ride.

"Ah, this is the best time of the day," Myron said, signaling to her. "Join me, Kerri?"

Kerri sat down at the table with him, shyly turning her eyes out over the deep blue of the lake, feeling cooler just watching as a speedboat cut a snowy swath through the restless water. "It's very considerate of the guests to be lazy after lunch," she said.

"I hear you're going on the moonlight ride," he said.

Kerri nodded, wishing that he was going to be there too. "I'm really looking forward to it," she admitted.

"Wish we all could go along," Myron observed, "but I guess I'll be going up early in the truck to help your stepfather set up the grills and get everything ready."

"Well, at least you won't be stuck in the kitchen peeling potatoes," Kerri teased shyly.

"You aren't going to let me forget that, are you?" Myron asked.

"Four potatoes in an hour?" Kerri gibed.

"So I'm not exactly experienced in the kitchen," he admitted without rancor. "It got me promoted to the tennis courts, didn't it?"

"Did you plan that?" Kerri asked, instantly suspicious.

His chuckle was wicked. "You'll never know, will you?"

"Well, you may be lucky now," Kerri told him, "but when it gets hot—"

"The guests won't want to play either," Myron finished. "I'll probably end up back in the kitchen taking instruction in elementary potato peeling." His eyes gleamed. "Want to give me private lessons?"

Kerri giggled, not sure how to answer. She was both disappointed and relieved when LuAnn came around the corner of the lodge and stepped onto the terrace. "There you are," she said.

"Me or Myron?" Kerri asked.

"You, Kerri." The girl stopped and blushed, making Kerri feel guilty. "I was just wondering what horse you wanted?" she asked.

"Sit down a minute," Kerri invited, wanting to make up for embarrassing her. "We were just cooling off. The kitchen gets pretty warm with everybody running around trying to get things put away."

"I have to help Derrick," LuAnn murmured, then awkwardly dropped into a chair.

"You rest for five minutes, then I'll put my boots on and we'll both help him, okay?"

LuAnn nodded. "I have to pick up the guest register anyway," she admitted. "We have to know who's planning to ride so we know what horses to saddle."

"I don't know how your brother keeps track," Myron said. "The second day, he had everybody on horses. And from what they said, everybody was happy with his choice."

"Mr. Harriman has good stock," LuAnn answered. "That makes it easier."

"Are you looking forward to the moonlight ride?"

Myron asked. "I was just telling Kerri that I'm jealous."

"You might get a chance to ride back," LuAnn said. "Sometimes guests decide to come back in the car, and it's easier to let someone ride a horse than lead it back."

"Well, if anyone wants to trade their saddle for a car seat, send them my way," Myron told her, then got to his feet, stretching and yawning, his muscles rippling under the light shirt. "Well, I've got to go hit a few tennis balls for Mrs. Preston," he said. "See you all later."

"Bye now," Kerri called.

LuAnn sighed. "I didn't mean to interrupt," she said. "I didn't know you were out here with him."

"No problem," Kerri assured her. "We were just talking."

"I wish I could just sit and talk to him," LuAnn observed. "Whenever he looks at me, I forget my own name and everyone else's." She giggled.

"You did okay today, ah . . . Mary Lou?" Kerri teased, getting to her feet. "Why don't you get the guest list and I'll go see if I can fit my tired waitress feet into my cowboy boots."

"Meet you here," LuAnn agreed, grinning.

Kerri went inside, shaking her head. Sandy and Lucille made her feel just the way LuAnn said she felt around Myron, she realized; yet she'd been able to make LuAnn feel better, and Myron . . . For some reason, Myron made her feel almost at ease in spite of his disgustingly good looks.

Things at the corral seemed to be in confusion by the time she reached there; but with LuAnn's help and Derrick's shouted instructions, they finished catching the horses required for the ride and set about matching bridles and saddles to horses and riders. Only when all the guest horses were tied to the corral, did Derrick come over and ask, "You want Sky Writer again, Kerri?"

Kerri considered for a moment, then nodded, her confidence strong after her afternoon meeting with Myron. "She was fine on our first ride."

Derrick's expression told her that he disapproved, but he said nothing, so Kerri went into the corral to get the mare. Her spirits lifted as the dainty creature left the other horses to come over and nuzzle her shoulder as she snapped the leadrope onto her halter. It was obvious that Sky Writer liked her as much as she liked the mare. Once she was saddled and tied with the others, Kerri returned to the shade of the stable roof, sinking down on the log there to wait with LuAnn and Derrick.

"So, what am I supposed to do on this ride?" she asked.

"Just watch the guests," Derrick answered with a slow smile that lit his well-tanned face. "I'll be leading and LuAnn will ride drag, so you take a spot in the middle. Make sure that everyone is doing all right; that their horses are keeping up; that they're comfortable with them. And keep an eye on the horses, too. Watch for any signs of lameness or any horse that doesn't appear to be acting quite right."

"If you think something is wrong, come back and get me," LuAnn said. "We don't like to stop the whole group unless it's really necessary, so if there's a small problem, you can trade places with me while I check it out."

Kerri nodded. "That sounds simple enough."

Derrick laughed. "When you get about two dozen inexperienced riders on horseback on a mountain trail, nothing is simple, believe me."

"Derrick always expects the worst," LuAnn said. "We never have any trouble that way."

"You just keep an eye on that Murphy kid," Derrick ordered. "He has delusions of competence, and he's liable to decide he's the Lone Ranger or something." His dark eyes met hers and Kerri could feel the warmth behind them. It was a strange feeling, exciting, yet reassuring at the same time.

She tried to find something to say, something that would let him know that she'd understood what was in his gaze, but before she could, LuAnn got to her feet. "Here they come," she announced, ending the moment. "Time to hit the dusty trail."

Derrick's fingers brushed hers as he went by, but he said nothing; and in a moment Kerri too was busy matching horses and riders according to his instructions. It seemed chaotic, but in a few minutes they were all mounted and Derrick was leading them past the lodge as they headed along the lakeshore for a little way, then turned into the trees.

Kerri stared longingly after him, wishing that she could be a guest and ride with him. Then she sighed and reined Sky Writer into the line just behind Billy Murphy. Mrs. Foster, a terribly timid rider, was directly behind her, so she felt she was close enough to handle what appeared to be the most likely problems on the trail.

They'd ridden for nearly an hour without mishap, and Kerri was feeling more and more relaxed. Sky Writer was an alert horse, but she seemed steady enough; and the wonderful vistas of pines and of the blue lake below them claimed her attention. The trail widened as they neared the top of a ridge, and Kerri looked away from the lake into the trees.

"Oh, look at the deer," she called as a doe and fawn moved away from the riders.

"I'm going to catch it," Billy Murphy shouted, reining the peaceful gelding off the trail and into the trees.

For a moment, Kerri was too startled to react; then she realized the treacherousness of the pine-needle-coated ground the boy was racing over. "Billy, you stop!" she shouted, urging Sky Writer into the forest after him, dimly conscious of his mother's shrieks behind her.

The boy, paying no attention, whipped the horse with his reins, guiding him deeper into the forest in pursuit of the deer. Kerri's heart nearly stopped as she saw the old horse stumble. Luckily, he recovered without spilling the boy, but the near-fall had jerked the reins from Billy's hands and he was now calling for help.

"Shut up and sit still," Kerri ordered, not caring what the other guests thought. "He'll stop if you quit yelling and bouncing around."

To her surprise, the boy obeyed, and in a moment the horse halted. She rode Sky Writer alongside, collecting the trailing reins. "That was very stupid," she told the boy. "You could have hurt yourself or your horse."

She turned the mare and led the gelding back up the rough hillside to where the rest of the riders waited. Only when he was safely in line behind his mother did she let him take the reins again—and then only after another stern lecture about the dangers of doing things suddenly on a trail ride.

LuAnn rode up beside her as Derrick started out

again. "You okay, Kerri?" she asked. "You want to ride drag for a while?"

"I'm fine," Kerri assured her. "It happened so fast I didn't even have time to get scared."

"Well, you did just the right thing," LuAnn told her. "Mr. Harriman is going to be really proud of you."

"I'm just glad nobody got hurt." Kerri patted Sky Writer's neck and reined her into line as LuAnn rode back along the string of horses.

"You were very brave," Mrs. Foster told her. "I didn't think you'd ever be able to stop that horse."

Kerri smiled at her and began telling her just how easy it was to control a horse if you just understood it. She felt very much a part of the crew now, and it was a good feeling. She could hardly wait till they reached the end of the ride so she could tell her mother that she'd proved herself.

The site of the steak fry was a surprise to Kerri. She'd expected to eat in one of the small grassy clearings in the mountains, but as the sun dropped lower in the sky, they left the high trails and began wending their way back down to the lower reaches, emerging onto a stretch of rocky shore at about five thirty.

Smiles and waves greeted them from the four big grills and the portable tables. "It's about time you got here," Perry called. "We were going to start the steaks and see if the smell would bring you down out of the hills."

"That would've done it," Derrick told him as he dismounted and moved to help some of the guests to the ground, assuring them as he did so that they'd feel better after they ate.

Kerri hurried to help him, taking a half-dozen horses and leading them away from the shore to a small grassy area between the shore and the pines. Once there, she unsaddled the horses and turned them loose, smiling at the eager way they began to graze. Though they were fed oats and hay daily, they all seemed to prefer the grass they found on the rides.

Once the horses were all taken care of, she, LuAnn and Derrick joined the line of people near the grills, sniffing hungrily. "There's something special about this," Derrick said. "No matter how good the food is in the dining room, it always tastes better out here after a long ride."

"It's so beautiful here, too," Kerri agreed, looking out over the lake, which was beginning to be shadowed as the sun sank.

"Eat with me, Kerri?" Derrick invited softly.

"I'd like that," Kerri told him as they loaded their big tin pie plates with the roasted potatoes and vegetables, coleslaw and garlic bread. Then they selected the steak that was done properly for their tastes.

Once they had collected the bandana-print napkins and sweat-beaded plastic glasses of lemonade, Kerri followed Derrick away from the group. He didn't say anything to her, but when he looked over his shoulder to make sure that she was following, his grin made her feel good and she didn't mind the walk away from the crowd.

"This is my favorite spot in this area," he said when they reached a large, flat rock about twenty feet above the shore. "The wind always comes from this angle, so the smoke goes away from us and we have the best view of anybody."

"Wow!" Kerri sank down on the sun-warmed rock

and stared off to the distance, where she could now see the toy-sized docks at the town. Little boats sped across the lake, their motors sounding like the drone of angry bees. Graceful sailboats moved like a silent ballet orchestrated by the wind, crossing from shadow to sunlight, their sails filled by the ever present breeze.

"You were great out there today," Derrick said, dropping beside her and attacking his food. "That could have been bad."

"I was scared to death when the horse stumbled," Kerri admitted.

"I may put the little monster on a different horse next time," Derrick told her. "Poco is too old for that kind of treatment."

"Sky Writer was fine," Kerri murmured, sipping her lemonade between bites of the delicious food.

"When she's good, she's very, very good; when she's bad, she's dangerous." Derrick's dark eyes met hers, and the sadness in his gaze kept her from getting angry or even leaping to the defense of the mare.

"Couldn't you and LuAnn be wrong?" Kerri asked. "I mean, maybe it'll never happen again, and Sky Writer will be just the way she is now."

Derrick shrugged.

"I think she deserves a second chance," Kerri continued, not liking to argue with Derrick but determined to keep riding the sweet-tempered mare.

"You're giving it to her," was his answer.

Swallowing a sigh, Kerri decided to change the subject. "Do you ever get bored with this?" she asked, gesturing at the whole busy scene below them on the shore. "I mean, it's all new to me, but you've been doing this for . . . how long?"

"I've been helping Mr. Harriman ever since he

started, but I've just been working as wrangler since last year. Before that, Mr. Harriman did all the guiding himself."

"Do you get tired of it?" Kerri repeated.

"Once in a while I'd like to tell everybody to take a flying leap in the lake, but most of the time it's okay. I love to ride and I like to show people around the area, so getting paid for it is really neat. I'll be able to buy a car this summer, and next year I can save most of my salary for college."

They ate in silence for several minutes, and Kerri could feel her nerves growing tense. She wanted to be able to talk to Derrick, to get to know him better, but there was something so serious about him. It had been, she thought with surprise, easier to talk to Myron. She couldn't help wondering why.

"What about you?" Derrick asked. "Do you think you'll get bored?"

Kerri swallowed hard, not sure how she could answer that question. Finally she shrugged. "I haven't even seen most of the area," she answered, then changed the subject again, asking him about the ride back.

"I'm betting we'll have quite a few that don't make the ride back," he said with a grin.

"What do you mean?"

"It's a long ride up here, and most of these people haven't done much riding. They'll be pretty sore by the time they sit around on the ground for an hour or so."

"Myron said he'd like to ride back if there's a horse available," Kerri told him.

"He'll have to check that with Mr. Harriman," Derrick answered, but his eyes changed as they met hers.

They sat in silence for several more minutes, eating the well-cooked steaks and sipping their lemonade. Finally, however, Derrick squirmed a little and asked, "Would you like to go into town to a movie tomorrow night, Kerri?"

"Ah . . . I . . . well, gosh, I'd have to ask Mom," she began, her heartbeat quickening with excitement at the thought.

"My folks said I could have the car. We'll have to take LuAnn too, but we can go over to Dickerson's and dance to the jukebox afterward if you like." Derrick's eyes were on the lake, not her, yet Kerri could feel the tension in his body as he waited for her answer.

"I'd love to go," Kerri managed to say. "I'll ask Mom when we go down for our dessert."

"You ready for that yet?" Derrick asked, his expression relaxing as he faced her again.

"I keep thinking that the watermelon sounds heavenly," Kerri began, "but I'm so full."

"It's mostly water," he said, getting to his feet and offering her a hand.

Kerri groaned. "I don't think the guests are the only ones feeling the results of this ride," she told him.

"You aren't going to ride back in the truck, are you?" Derrick asked, stopping so suddenly she nearly crashed into him.

"No. I'll be okay once I get on Sky Writer," Kerri assured him. "I just wish we could ride together sometime."

"I'll see what I can do," Derrick promised with a grin. "You go talk to your Mom about tomorrow night."

Kerri opened her mouth to ask him what he meant,

but before she could say anything, he'd left her side, heading for the grills, where Bob was still fussing with the coals and taking the last of the food out of its wrappings. A quick look around showed her that her mother was over near the lapping lake, cutting wedges of melon.

"Having fun, Kerri?" she asked the moment Kerri reached her.

"It's terrific," Kerri replied.

"I saw you and Derrick going off together," her mother went on, efficiently producing wedges of watermelon and placing them on plates. "He's a nice boy, Kerri."

"I'm glad you think so," Kerri told her with a grin, "since he's asked me to go to a show with him tomorrow night. May I go?"

"Into Whitefish?" Her mother's tone was less enthusiastic.

"He said we'd be taking LuAnn too," Kerri assured her, well aware that her mother hadn't thought about her dating, since she'd never had the chance until just the last month or so before she left Spokane.

"Well, I suppose it will be all right," her mother admitted. "Do you want some watermelon?"

"Thanks. And yes, we do." Kerri couldn't keep from smiling so widely that, she was sure, everyone must suspect what was going on.

"You're kind of exclusive, aren't you?" Myron asked, coming up behind her. "Does going on the ride make you too good to eat with the common staff?"

"It was just so nice and cool up there," Kerri murmured, aware that she was blushing.

"Trust the experienced man to find the best spots," Myron teased.

"Did you find a horse to ride back?" Kerri asked, mainly because she wanted to change the subject.

"Don't know yet, but I've put my bid in." He grinned at her. "I hear you were a heroine your first time out."

"What?" Her mother asked before Kerri could answer.

"Oh, it wasn't that much," Kerri answered, then explained what had happened, finishing, "That's why we were a little late getting here."

"I hope nothing like that happens on the way back," her mother said.

"It won't," Kerri assured her. "Everyone will be too full and lazy to do anything dumb."

"Well, here's your watermelon," her mother said, handing her two plates.

Myron lifted one bushy golden eyebrow; but before he could say anything, Derrick joined them, claiming his plate. "Mr. Harriman is looking for you, Myron," he said, then turned his questioning gaze to Kerri.

"I can go," Kerri answered his unspoken question.

"Great."

Several of the guests came to the small table to get more watermelon, so Derrick took her hand and gently led her away, following the edge of the water for a short distance before turning inland to climb once again to their rock. "I can ride with you going back," he said as they settled themselves together on the hard surface. "Mr. Harriman is going to lead the group down."

"How come?" Kerri was surprised.

"Several of the guests have already told him they don't want to ride back, so that means lots of extra horses. He's even going to ask your Mom, I think. At least he was checking to see if there was a gentle horse free, and he sure doesn't have to worry about what he rides."

"Everything seems to be working out," Kerri observed, leaning back against the still-warm cliff face.

"It's going to be a beautiful night," Derrick agreed.

It was almost dark by the time they started saddling the horses for the ride back to the lodge. The guests who'd chosen to return to the lodge in cars had already left—as had most of the staff. Kerri mounted Sky Writer and watched as Myron tossed the last bag of garbage into the back of the truck, then walked over to where LuAnn was holding the reins of a chestnut.

Once Myron was mounted, he looked around. Kerri was aware of his gaze resting on her, though she was careful not to let him see that she was watching him. He studied her for several minutes, but when Bob called them to start, he didn't wait; he reined into line a few horses behind her mother, who was following Bob.

Kerri started to urge Sky Writer forward, but Derrick put a hand on her arm. "I told LuAnn that I'd ride drag," he said. "Hope you don't mind."

"Why should I?" Kerri asked, instantly aware that they would be virtually alone on the trail most of the time, since their only function was to make sure that none of the guests fell behind the group.

The moon was rising well, making a silver path on the lake, but once they rode into the forest, the darkness was nearly complete and Kerri couldn't help feeling a little apprehensive. She was glad Derrick was so close beside her that their knees brushed as the horses walked along. She offered no objection when he reached out and took her hand, and her heartbeat quickened as he leaned over and kissed her lightly.

"I'm real glad you came to Lakeside, Kerri," he whispered. Then his lips found hers again, and she felt that she was shivering inside.

"I'm glad too," she answered as the horses broke out of the shadow of the pines and into the bright silvery light of a meadow. Kerri looked ahead, shyly watching the riders in front of them as they crossed the grass and then disappeared into the shadows again. The night was magic, and she felt as pretty and exciting as she'd always dreamed of being. She hoped the ride would never end.

Once they reached the lodge, however, the magic flowed away. The guests were tired, and some of them were cranky as they dismounted and headed for their rooms or cabins, leaving the tired horses to be cared for. Kerri, her own body tender from the long ride, swallowed a sigh and set to work to help unsaddle, clean and feed the animals.

By the time the last horse had been turned into the proper corral, she didn't mind the short "good night" she got from Derrick and LuAnn; she was interested only in a hot bath and her own bed. Still, when Derrick said, "See you tomorrow," she felt better. It was a date, a real one, not just a casual foursome formed with friends. She longed to write and tell Donna all about it.

6

The next day dragged, and by the time the kitchen was cleaned up after the evening meal, Kerri was a bundle of nerves. She tried on everything in her closet, not sure what she should wear into town.

"I should've asked LuAnn," she told herself angrily, then shook her head. She hadn't even mentioned the evening to LuAnn, though they'd met twice during the time after lunch.

"Would you like some help?" her mother asked from the doorway.

Kerri nodded, embarrassed by the way she'd spread her clothes all over the room. "I'm having trouble making up my mind what to wear," she admitted.

"You're just going to a movie?"

"Well, he said something about going to Dickerson's to dance afterward, so—" Kerri stopped. "I don't even know what that is."

"Dickerson's is a drugstore, the 'teen hangout' in

town," her mother supplied. "It really isn't much of a drugstore, but it has a huge area in back where there's a jukebox and room to dance." She pawed through the dresses and slack sets on the bed, finally selecting a rather plain green print. "This looks about right," she said.

"Really?" Kerri studied it. The dress had a wide, round neck and was sleeveless, which made it rather bare.

"With this," her mother continued, picking up the small white jacket. "And this." She added a matching green scarf. "White shoes and you'll look like you stepped right out of a magazine."

"Not too dressy?" Kerri was skeptical.

"I haven't been in there in the evenings too often, but the times I have been, this is pretty much the way the girls were dressed."

"Terrific," Kerri told her. "Thanks a lot."

"I want you to have a good time here," her mother told her. "Going to Dickerson's with Derrick is the perfect way for you to meet more of the young people you'll be going to school with this fall."

Kerri nodded, then turned her back, lifting her hair so her mother could zip the dress for her. "I just hope I make a good impression," she said.

"You will. You already have with the kids on the staff, so the ones in town should be easy."

"Well, I—" Kerri began, but a tap on her door interrupted her.

"There's a handsome young man waiting out in the lobby," Bob announced when she invited him in. "He bears a slight resemblance to our wrangler; but I don't think old cowboy Derrick would be so slicked up."

"Bob," her mother murmured in warning.

Bob laughed. "Shall I tell him you're about ready?"

Kerri nodded, suddenly too anxious and excited to speak.

"About five minutes," her mother told him.

"I'll tell him she's worth the wait," Bob promised, leaving.

Kerri swallowed hard.

"He won't tease him," her mother assured her. "He just cares a great deal about both of you."

Kerri nodded, grateful, but unable to say anything yet. She turned to the mirror and gave her auburn waves a quick brushing, then checked her lipstick one last time. That done, there was nothing left to do but pick up her small white clutch purse and follow her mother out to the busy lobby where Derrick was waiting.

The good-byes were mercifully brief, and it wasn't till they stepped out into the still-bright air of early evening that she thought to ask, "Where is LuAnn?"

"I dropped her off at the stable," Derrick answered.

"Isn't she going with us?"

"Sure she is. She just wanted to check on Pussy Foot. She came in lame today and LuAnn couldn't find anything wrong at the time, so she wanted to see if her leg had swollen since."

"Horses, horses, horses," Kerri observed with a giggle.

"Well, in this case, it's understandable. Pussy Foot was LuAnn's first horse. Mr. Harriman bought her from Dad when LuAnn outgrew her." Derrick grinned. "Besides, this is horse country. You think LuAnn is bad, wait till you meet the rest of the Junior Ridge Riders."

Kerri said nothing, aware that she was always concerned about Sky Writer and remembering only too well how awful she'd felt when her favorite mount had suddenly disappeared from the riding stable in Spokane. She'd wanted so badly to know who bought him and how he was doing, but no one was able or willing to tell her, so she'd never known for sure what happened to him.

"Is something wrong?" Derrick asked, making her realize that she hadn't said a word since they reached the car.

"I was just thinking about horses," Kerri answered, "and how much you can come to care about them."

"Sky Writer?" His tone was very neutral.

"And a couple of horses I rode a lot at the stable in Spokane," Kerri acknowledged. "Sometimes there is just a special feeling that you have."

Derrick nodded as he started the car, but he didn't say anything. Kerri knew it was because he still didn't approve of her riding and caring about Sky Writer. Words of defense for the mare rose in her throat, but she said nothing, aware that it would do no good. Her feelings for the friendly pinto weren't going to change his mind.

LuAnn came out of the stable as they drew up in front of it. "How is she?" Derrick asked as she climbed into the car, forcing Kerri to move over closer to Derrick.

"There's no sign of swelling or tenderness in the leg, so it must just be a stone bruise to her hoof. Her hoof looks okay, though; but she's still not putting much weight on that leg."

"I'll check her in the morning," Derrick promised. "Now let's forget horses and think about the movie." He named the picture. "I hope you haven't seen it," he added. "I forgot that it might have played in Spokane before it came here."

"I missed it," Kerri assured him, and their eyes met. A spark seemed to fly between them and she caught her breath nervously. "I've always wanted to see it."

It was, she decided, going to be a simply super evening. She looked ahead at the road that twisted between the tall pines and smiled.

The movie was great. Kerri and Derrick left the theater feeling so good Kerri was almost dancing as they walked along the sidewalk toward the winking neon sign that marked Dickerson's as one of the few places still open this late in the evening. It wasn't an imposing building. The paint was chipped near the door, and the window displays looked more neglected than inviting. However, when Derrick opened the door, the beat of the jukebox seemed to reach out to greet them.

"You guys go ahead," LuAnn said. "I'm going to see if the new *Western Horseman* magazine is in." She headed for the magazine and paperback racks on one side of the room.

Kerri looked around at the old-fashioned counters with their displays of cosmetics and costume jewelry. Just ahead of them was a rather large horseshoe-shaped fountain and snack bar; and beyond it she could see the dance floor her mother had described. At the moment, it was very much occupied by about twenty dancing couples.

Tables and booths surrounded the dance floor, and Derrick led her to the closest empty booth. "What would you like?" he asked. "Soda? Milkshake? A hamburger?"

"What are you having?" Kerri asked.

"They make a terrific chocolate-cherry milkshake,"

Derrick answered. "I always have one when I'm in town."

"That sounds super," Kerri said. "I've never had one."

"Be right back." Derrick left her to go to the fountain, which Kerri now realized was self-service for the rear area, though a single young boy was clearing the tables from time to time.

"Watching the competition?" Josie Snyder asked, making Kerri jump nervously.

"Oh, hi. I was just thinking that I like working in our dining room better," Kerri said as the older girl slipped into the booth opposite her.

"The crowd here is more fun," Josie told her, "but I prefer Lakeside, too. What are you doing in exciting and colorful downtown Whitefish?"

"Derrick brought me in to a movie."

"Ah ha, smart guy," Josie said. "Getting in ahead of the competition."

"Oh come on," Kerri murmured, embarrassed yet pleased at Josie's estimate of the situation. "LuAnn is with us, so . . ." She let it trail off, then asked, "How about you? Do you come down here every night, or are you on a date?"

"Just checking out the crowd," Josie answered. "Perry's around here somewhere. He met this girl who's staying at the Bay Point cabins and she comes here pretty often, so he has to stop off here just about every night." She shook her head. "In the summer we meet a lot of the tourist kids here, but in the winter it's pretty much just our own place. Everybody comes here after school, and Don keeps it open for us Saturday and Sunday nights, too."

"Hi, Josie," Derrick said, arriving with the

milkshakes. "Can I get you something?" He set the big glasses down and slid in beside Kerri.

"No thanks. I've got my order over there." Josie pointed to a table across the dance floor, where Kerri could see Perry talking to a very pretty brunette. "I'm going back. I just thought I'd keep Kerri company while you were getting your drinks. Where's LuAnn, by the way?"

"Last I saw her, she was getting a magazine," Derrick answered.

Josie nodded, then slipped out of the booth, leaving them alone. Kerri watched as she made her way to the front of the drugstore and smiled as she came back with LuAnn. "She's very nice, isn't she?" she asked.

Derrick nodded. "She and Perry are great. In fact, most of the kids are pretty neat. You'll like them, Kerri."

"Oh, I—" Kerri began, but before she could go on, two boys slid into the booth opposite them, demanding to be introduced. They were followed by others, male and female, throughout the rest of the evening. Kerri tried to remember the names, but she soon lost track and was unable to remember any of them.

After about an hour, Myron appeared at the table. "How about letting me borrow the little lady, Derrick?" he asked.

Derrick's eyes met hers, and when Kerri made no objections, he slid out and let her go. "So the wrangler got his bid in first, huh?" Myron commented as they moved into the crowd on the dance floor.

"What do you mean?" Kerri asked.

Myron laughed. "That I should have ridden back with you last night, that's all."

Kerri tossed her head, the implied flattery making

her glow. "I thought you were pretty busy with the Pendergast girl," she told him, thinking of the resort guest he'd been playing tennis with that afternoon.

"She's fourteen," he answered.

Kerri laughed. "Funny how she only acts twenty-one."

He nodded. "She's cute enough to get away with it."

The beat of the music quickened, and Kerri had to concentrate as he began a new series of steps and spins. She was dimly aware that several of the couples had left the floor; but it wasn't till the music stopped that she realized they were alone on the dance floor. The clapping brought the blood to her cheeks as Myron led her back to the booth where LuAnn now sat reading her magazine and drinking a milkshake while Derrick talked to one of the boys.

"We'll show them at the dance Saturday night," Myron told her as Derrick got up to let her back into the booth.

Derrick said nothing, but Kerri sensed that he was annoyed. She finished her milkshake without looking his way. She waited till Derrick had finished his conversation with the blond boy, then looked up at the clock above the jukebox. "Do you think we should go pretty soon?" she asked. "I did tell Mom I'd be home before midnight."

"One dance?" Derrick asked. "Or am I too tame for you?"

Kerri forced a smile. "I'd love to dance with you, Derrick," she told him, "and I like the way you dance."

"I'm not in Myron's league."

"Neither am I," Kerri admitted. "I've never danced like that."

"You looked terrific." The compliment was grudging.

"He's a super dancer, that's all."

Derrick's arm tightened just a little around her waist and he spun her quickly, but he said nothing. Kerri swallowed a sigh, not sure how to handle the situation. She'd never had anyone jealous of her before.

Once out in the car, Kerri was glad when LuAnn started talking about an article in her magazine. She needed time to think, Kerri realized, time to decide how to act with both Myron and Derrick. For a moment she wished that Donna were still living just two blocks away. Whom could she ask? The only one of the girls here that she felt she could trust was Josie, yet how could she confide her lack of experience to someone she'd known such a short time?

"Tired?" Derrick asked, breaking into her thoughts.

Kerri started nervously, realizing that they were nearly back to the lodge and that she'd been too busy with her own thoughts to enter the conversation. "I guess I am," she murmured. "We start so early every morning and keep so busy."

"You're just not used to being on a ranch," LuAnn informed her. "We get up at five every morning, winter and summer."

Kerri groaned at the thought.

Derrick laughed. "Don't listen to her," he advised. "She used to hide her head under the pillow till seven when it was cold."

The bantering between brother and sister lifted her spirits, and she managed to keep up with them till they reached the lodge. Derrick parked in the lot, then got out to walk her around to the rear door where the terrace lay in shadow.

"It was terrific having you with us tonight, Kerri," he told her, stopping near the door.

"I had a wonderful time," Kerri answered, meaning it. "Thank you for taking me."

"We'll have to do it again soon," he continued. "Maybe we could go to the rodeo some afternoon."

"What about the rides?" Kerri asked.

"We all get one day a week off," Derrick reminded her. "We'll just have to work it out so we have the same day off." He stopped, then added, "And on a day when there is a rodeo in the area."

"How do we do that?" Kerri inquired.

"Well, let me check on the rodeo schedules, then we can work from that, okay?"

"Sounds super to me," Kerri answered. "I've never been to a rodeo."

"No question, we've got to improve your education." His arm tightened around her shoulders and he pulled her close.

Kerri felt her heartbeat quicken as she looked up at him. His face was a pale blur in the darkness. His eyes caught the light as he looked down at her. He was going to kiss her, she realized. She didn't want to pull away or speak and ruin the magic of the moment. Instead, she stood very still, her lips slightly parted.

He bent his head slowly till their lips met. She wanted the kiss to go on forever, yet she was somewhat relieved when he released her. The rush of emotions she felt was almost frightening.

"See you tomorrow," he whispered, his voice sounding slightly hoarse.

"Thanks for the nice evening," Kerri called after

him, suddenly cold and lonely even before he disappeared around the corner of the building. She stayed where she was till she heard his car starting.

The moment she opened the door and stepped into the kitchen, the lights were turned on and her mother appeared in the doorway to the apartment. "Did you have a good time, honey?" she asked.

Kerri felt the red rising in her cheeks at the memory of Derrick's kiss, but she managed to smile and nod. "It was neat."

"Did you meet a lot of people?" her mother continued the quiz.

"Tons." Kerri edged her way toward the door. It wasn't that she didn't want to tell her mother about the evening or that she had anything to hide, it was just too new to share. "I'm really tired," she murmured over her shoulder. "And I have to be up so early tomorrow."

Her mother smiled gently. "I'm glad it was fun," she said. "See you in the morning."

"Good night." Kerri fled to her room.

Once she was ready for bed, however, she found sleep elusive. The whole evening unfolded in her mind. She felt again the closeness she'd shared with Derrick, then the excitement of Myron's presence and the way they'd danced together. Tomorrow afternoon she'd write and tell Donna everything, she promised herself. So much had happened since her first letter. By then, she thought, maybe she'd be able to figure out what she was going to do.

Saturdays were always busy. The empty cabins were filled by arriving families. Everyone seemed to be having problems. Rooms weren't ready; guests were confused by the various rules and regulations; even the day's ride was late leaving as Derrick had to wait for several riders.

It was nearly time to start work on the evening meal—which, much like her welcoming party, was to be a barbecue on the terrace followed by dancing—before Kerri finally had a moment to herself. She wandered through the living quarters, remembering the letter she'd planned to write.

When she went to get her stationery and a pen, however, she found an envelope that someone had placed on her dresser while she was busy elsewhere. Her hands shook a little as she opened it.

"Dear Kerri," Donna had written . . .

I can't believe your luck. Myron Fuller is the dreamiest boy I've ever seen. No wonder you're crazy about him. I showed the picture to everybody and they are all green—even Jamie.

Have you dated him yet? What do you do besides go horseback riding and swimming and all that neat stuff? I can hardly wait. Do you realize that I'll be there in just two weeks? Do you think you'll be able to find me someone to date? I realize it won't be Myron, but some of the other boys in the picture are cute, too.

Kerri read on as Donna filled her in on all the local activities. It made good reading, but even as she finished the letter, she realized that it wasn't the same. She missed her old gang of friends, but she was also very eager for the evening's activities.

She thought about what Donna had said about Myron and swallowed a sigh, wondering how to tell her friend that she wasn't really dating Myron. She'd hardly mentioned Derrick in her first letter, she realized, and he hadn't exactly been noticeable in the pictures her mother had taken at the party.

"Hey Kerri, how about giving us a hand?" her mother called from the kitchen. Kerri folded the letter and put it into the drawer.

"Later," she promised herself, thinking even as she did so that she might have more to write about when the evening was over.

The terrace looked very festive. The boys had hung Japanese lanterns, and the tables were covered with bright new cloths.

"Not quite the same as it was the last time, is it?" Sandy asked, ladling beans onto the plates as Kerri dished up the salads.

"What do you mean?" Kerri asked.

"Last time you were guest of honor."

Kerri giggled. "I think serving is easier," she admitted. "I was scared to death meeting everyone for the first time."

"Didn't slow you up for long." Sandy smiled at the people they were serving, not even looking at Kerri.

"Huh?" Kerri forgot what she was doing for a moment and stared at the beautiful blonde.

"I'd like some potato salad," an impatient voice intruded, forcing her attention back to the passing line of guests.

"What did you mean, Sandy?" Kerri asked when the line slowed for a moment.

"I saw you at Dickerson's last night."

"I didn't see you," Kerri observed. "Why didn't you come over and say hello?"

"I was in a hurry."

The crowd moved in again, claiming Kerri's attention, but her thoughts stayed on the blonde's words. There was something in her tone that made what she'd said important, but Kerri wasn't sure what it was.

Though she meant to ask Sandy about it again when they finished serving, the girl was already sitting with Myron and several of the guests by the time Kerri had filled her plate. Kerri looked around, hoping to spot LuAnn or Derrick, but the terrace was crowded, and since they weren't on the serving staff, they'd already found places at a distant table.

"Over here, Kerri," Josie called, waving.

Grateful, Kerri took her well-filled plate over and sat down in the one vacant chair at the table. "I'm starving," she moaned. "Smelling that meat all afternoon, then having to serve . . ."

"I know," Josie agreed. "I thought I'd never get all the drinks poured."

"At least everybody has to serve his own seconds," Perry observed, his blue eyes full of laughter. "Otherwise we'd all starve to death."

They ate in silence for several minutes, listening to the guests who shared the long table, talking about the afternoon ride and tomorrow's boat excursion around the lake. Then Josie turned to Kerri. "I'd watch my back for a while if I were you, Kerri," she said unexpectedly.

"What do you mean?" Kerri asked, putting down her fork.

"I saw you talking to Sandy in line, and she had her vulture smile."

"She was being weird," Kerri agreed. "She said something about my not being slow and then said she'd seen me last night. I tried to ask her what she meant, but she just ignored me and then we got busy and . . ." Kerri let it trail off. "Did you see her?"

"She came in while you and Myron were doing your floor show," Josie informed her. "She looked daggers for a couple of minutes, then split. I think she was looking for Myron."

"And she thought that I—" Kerri nodded, suddenly understanding. "Maybe I should've told her I was there with Derrick."

"When it comes to Mr. Myron Fuller, the great and gorgeous, it doesn't matter," Josie went on. "She won't go steady with him, but she sure doesn't like it when he looks at anyone else."

"Lay off Myron," Perry snapped. "He's an okay guy."

Josie laughed. "It's just that he can't help being irresistible."

Perry glared at her for a moment, then laughed too. "So, are you looking forward to tomorrow, Kerri?" he asked.

"What is it exactly?" Kerri inquired, welcoming the change of subject.

"The resort rents the big boat *Lake Belle* for the afternoon. We take our own food and staff along and we cruise all the way around the lake, serving a late lunch on the deck so everyone can eat while they admire the scenery."

"Are you going?" Kerri asked.

Perry shook his head. "I've been often enough. I'd rather use the time as an afternoon off. They only need four or five to serve. Everybody else just goes along for the trip. After this time, probably we'll draw straws or maybe set up a rotation schedule."

Perry started telling tales about last summer's boat

cruises. He kept the staff entertained till they'd finished their main course. Leaning back with a sigh, Josie observed, "We'd better get up there if we want any strawberry shortcake. That bunch is really hungry."

"I don't know where I'll put it, but after cleaning all those berries, I'm sure going to have some," Kerri told her, getting up and heading for the table.

"Oh Kerri, there you are." Sandy came up just as she was ladling strawberries onto her shortcake.

"What can I do for you, Sandy?" Kerri asked without much enthusiasm.

"Nothing for me," Sandy answered with a warm smile that didn't reach her innocent blue eyes. "It's Myron. Strawberry shortcake is his favorite, and I was going to fix one for him; but Mrs. O'Roarke just asked me to get a bunch of stuff from the kitchen, so I was wondering if you'd do it. He likes it with gobs of whipped cream."

"Sure, no problem." Kerri set her dish down and began fixing a second one as Sandy walked away, heading across the terrace toward the kitchen. Preparing the second dessert took only a few minutes, and once she'd put whipped cream on both of them, she headed across the terrace to where Myron sat with several young men, his back to her.

"Hey, Myron," she said, "here's your strawberry short—" She let the words die as she started to set the heaped bowl down in front of him and realized that he was already eating a dessert.

"Wow, Myron, you've got some pull," one of the boys at the table taunted. "Good-looking girls keep bringing you food."

Kerri felt the heat rising in her cheeks as the words of explanation filled her throat, then choked her as she lifted her gaze from Myron's startled face to see Sandy standing on the far side of the terrace, watching and laughing.

"I . . . I guess I made a mistake," she managed. "I . . ."

"Well, if you don't want it, Myron, I'll take it," the other boy said. "I never turn down food."

Kerri was only dimly aware of setting both dishes on the table before she turned and hurried across the terrace, brushing roughly through the crowd. Her face was burning and she could feel angry tears rising in her eyes.

7

Kerri stopped when she reached the shadows beyond the terrace. Where could she go? The path to her room was blocked by guests and staff. There were guests wandering along the lakeshore and crisscrossing the lawn in various directions. Kerri looked longingly toward the distant darkness of the pines, then headed for the corrals, seeking a warm black-and-white shoulder to cry on.

Sky Writer seemed to sense her discomfort, sniffing at her shoulders companionably then turning to rub her head against Kerri's dress, leaving a few black and white hairs on the bright gold fabric.

"I wish I could spend more time with you," Kerri told her. "I know you'd like to go on the rides every day; but I only have a couple of free hours in the afternoon, and that's not long enough for us to ride very far."

She petted the mare, wondering what she should do. The thought of returning to the dance and the stares of everyone who'd seen her hasty departure made her cringe, yet how could she avoid it? She wasn't a guest, and there was still the cleaning-up to be done.

"What are you doing down here?" LuAnn's voice brought Kerri around at once, and she was grateful for the darkness that hid her.

"I just felt like a walk," Kerri lied, unable to admit the truth. "What are you doing here?"

"I came down to check on Pussy Foot." LuAnn's voice told Kerri that she wasn't telling the truth either.

"Is she all right?" Kerri asked.

"I haven't been inside yet."

"How is the party going?"

"Derrick's looking for you now the dancing is starting," LuAnn answered, walking toward the stable. "Are you going back?"

"I have to," Kerri replied. "I'm supposed to be helping with the cleanup."

"If you stay missing a little longer, they'll probably be done," LuAnn counseled.

"I'd better wash up in the tack room," Kerri continued, remembering that there was a water faucet in there. "I'm a little horsy for the kitchen."

"I'll go check Pussy Foot," LuAnn said, leaving her at the door of the stable.

Kerri hurried into the tack room, switching on the light, then cringing from the pain of her dry, burning eyes and flushed face. There was no mirror in the tack room, but a glance into the shiny side of a bit showed the marks of her tears. She spent several minutes bathing her face in cold water, hoping to erase the marks of her discomfiture.

After drying her face cautiously on the paper towels, she brushed the horsehair from her dress, smoothed her hair as best she could without a mirror's guidance, then went back out into the stable to look for LuAnn. She spotted her leaning over the stall door at the other end.

"You going back up to the terrace?" she asked.

"Not for a while," LuAnn answered without turning around.

"Is there something wrong with Pussy Foot?" Kerri asked.

"I think she's ready to be turned out with the others tomorrow."

Kerri opened her mouth to ask LuAnn why she wasn't going back, then stopped herself in time, remembering how lonely it could be in a crowd when you didn't have anyone special to be with. For a moment she wanted to stay with the girl, but her sense of duty was stronger; and she knew that her mother would be looking for her if she didn't go and do her share of the cleaning and the putting away of the food.

"I'd wait and walk back with you, but I've got to put in an appearance in the kitchen or Mom will have everybody out hunting for me," she told the younger girl. "When you do come back, sit with me, okay?"

"Thanks," LuAnn said, but she didn't look around. Kerri left reluctantly, wondering if the girl might be crying.

The scene on the terrace looked quite different as Kerri approached. The tables had been moved back to the fringes of the flagstones, leaving the center for dancing. Kerri slowed, not sure how to rejoin the group. She was sure that Sandy had seen her ignominious flight, and she was afraid that she had told the others.

Her doubts weren't helped by seeing Myron's blond head among those around the serving table. He had to think that she was running after him, she thought bitterly. He probably thought she was an idiot. Why hadn't she just smiled and walked away with the stupid extra dessert? Or she could have said something about being asked to bring it to him.

But she hadn't, she thought bitterly. She'd done just exactly what Sandy wanted her to—She'd run away like a scared and embarrassed child. Anger blazed through her as she watched the sexy blonde cross the terrace and say something to Myron.

Kerri took a deep breath and moved into the shadow of the building and went around to enter through the front door, crossing the nearly deserted lobby and making her way to the kitchen. There was a bit of teasing about her absence, but as soon as she settled down to work, it stopped. As she scraped plates and prepared the dishes for the dishwasher, Kerri stared straight ahead, her mind busy. Sandy wasn't going to get away with this, she decided. There had to be a way to make her pay for what she'd done.

"Well, well, look who's back helping." Sandy's voice was sweet and thick as honey as she came up beside Kerri.

Kerri, clumsy with returning anger, spun around—accidentally tipping the plate of leftover salad in Sandy's direction. The thick mixture of melted jello, potato salad, beans and greens, shifted and dropped, leaving a long, ugly stain all down the front of Sandy's blue-print peasant dress.

"Oh Sandy, I'm sorry," Kerri said aghast, her eyes meeting the blonde's. "You startled me."

Fury rose in the wide blue eyes, and for a moment Kerri thought the girl would explode at her. She braced herself, but Sandy seemed to gain control. Red burned in her face and her eyes blazed, but the full lips remained pressed together.

"Would you like me to see if I can rinse some of that off?" Kerri offered as she wiped the spilled food off the floor with a paper towel.

"Thanks, but you've done quite enough." Sandy turned and stamped out of the kitchen, heading toward the front of the lodge.

There was a moment of stunned silence in the kitchen, then Josie coughed slightly and said, "Gee, Kerri, you'll probably have to do all the rest of Sandy's work tonight."

The laughter that followed went a long way toward healing the pain Kerri had been feeling earlier, though she still dreaded the moment when she'd have to face Myron again. She went back to work on the huge stack of dishes, feeling much better.

Because she wasn't that eager to see Myron, Kerri stayed in the kitchen till everything was finished and even Mrs. O'Roarke had collected her purse from under the cupboard and left for the day. She was just putting the day's collection of dishcloths, towels and rags into the laundry basket when the rear door opened and Myron came in.

"So this is where you've been hiding," he observed, putting three more glasses on the drain board.

"Where did you get those?" Kerri asked, avoiding his eyes by concentrating on the glasses.

"I've been checking the shrubbery," Myron

answered. "Now. What are you doing hiding in here, Kerri?"

"I took a little walk and was late getting back to help, so I thought I should make up for it." Kerri could feel his gray eyes searching her face, but she was afraid to look up at him, afraid of the mockery she might see in his expression.

"How come you didn't stay to help eat up that shortcake?" he asked.

"I suddenly discovered I wasn't hungry." The flip words came out of nowhere, surprising her.

"Did someone tell you to bring me that dessert?"

Kerri nodded.

"Sandy?"

Kerri finally looked up. The gray eyes were dancing, but not with mockery. She nodded once again.

"Where is she?"

"She had a little accident, and I guess she went home to change. I don't know if she's planning to come back." Kerri couldn't keep the note of triumph from sounding in her voice.

Myron leaned against the cupboard, his eyes narrowed as he studied her. "You wouldn't have had anything to do with that accident, would you?" he asked.

Kerri looked down at her feet. "I can be so clumsy sometimes," she admitted.

Myron's laughter filled the kitchen. Suddenly his hands closed around her waist and she felt herself lifted into the air. "Kerri, Kerri, Kerri, there is a side to you I never suspected," he told her. Then suddenly she was in his arms and his lips were seeking hers.

Her pulse quickened as he held her tighter and kissed her with a demanding pressure that both excited and frightened her. She wanted to pull away as the kiss deepened, yet she seemed unable to do anything about it.

A sound broke the spell. Kerri started and pulled away, shaken by the conflicting feelings that raced through her. She turned to see Derrick standing by the door.

"Excuse me," Derrick said coldly, "I didn't mean to interrupt anything." He turned on his heel and left before Kerri had a chance to say a word.

"Oops," Myron murmured with a chuckle.

Kerri opened her mouth, but no words came out. She took a step toward the door, then hesitated, wanting to go after Derrick but not sure what she could say even if she did catch up with him.

"Ready to go out and dance?" Myron asked, forcing her attention back to him.

"I . . . I guess so," Kerri answered. This was it, her moment of triumph, and all she felt was . . . was what? She realized that she honestly wasn't sure what she felt. "Just let me put those glasses in the sink," she murmured. "It's too late for the dishwasher."

"We'll have more by morning," Myron told her. "Mr. Harriman runs a busy bar out there."

Unable to think up another excuse, she followed obediently when he took her hand and led her out into the coolness of the evening. He moved directly onto the dance floor, where the phonograph was playing a dreamy waltz.

Myron's arm was strong and warm, but she couldn't relax the way she had before. Only when she finally closed her eyes and stopped looking for Derrick's face in the crowd was she truly able to enjoy the dancing.

It was almost half an hour before she felt she could excuse herself from the table she and Myron were sharing with Perry, Josie and three of the guests. She made her way across the terrace to where her mother was helping her stepfather at the makeshift bar.

"Have you seen Derrick and LuAnn?" she asked as casually as she could.

"Oh, they left, honey," her mother answered. "Almost an hour ago, I guess."

"Left?" Kerri couldn't hide her feeling of disappointment.

"He was looking for you, and I told him you were probably in the kitchen. Didn't he find you?" Her mother looked concerned. "When he said good night, I was going to ask him, but I was busy, so—"

"He found me," Kerri answered, turning away.

"Did he—" Her mother stopped as several of the guests came to claim her attention. Kerri gave her what she hoped was a reassuring wave and started slowly across the flagstones to where Myron and the others waited. Myron smiled lazily at her as she slipped back into her chair. "We were just talking about tomorrow," he said. "Are you on the serving list for the boat trip?"

Kerri nodded. "I'm not taking any time off till my friend Donna gets here. I'm working for Lucille tomorrow." She paused, then asked, "How about you?"

His gray eyes narrowed slightly. "I wouldn't miss it for the world."

It was nearly an hour before the crowd began to thin and Kerri and Josie excused themselves to begin clearing the glasses from the tables. The boys helped Bob dismantle the now-cool barbecue equipment and put away the tables.

"I got to hand it to you," Josie said as they reached the quiet kitchen. "I think you've really done it."

"Done what?" Kerri asked, noticing the coolness in the older girl's voice.

"Succeeded where the rest of the girls haven't been able to."

"I don't know what you mean," Kerri persisted.

"I think Myron really likes you," Josie continued. "At least, Sandy must think so to pull an old trick like that extra dessert."

Kerri felt the red rising in her cheeks. "I felt like an idiot," she confessed.

"You got your revenge quickly enough," Josie pointed out.

"That was an accident," Kerri protested.

"It got you what you wanted," Josie answered. "But, Kerri, remember that Myron will be going away to college in a couple of months, and I don't think he's ever gone steady with anyone for more than a month."

"Oh come on, just because—" Kerri began, but before she could go on, Perry came in with another load of dishes and there was no further opportunity. All too soon, she was bidding everyone a laughing good-bye.

Only when she was alone did she have time to think and to wonder about what had happened. The kiss she'd shared in the kitchen filled her mind, and for a moment she savored the wild excitement it had brought her; then that faded and Derrick's face was before her.

There had been hurt in his dark eyes and shock on his face—that much she remembered only too clearly. But what should she have done? she asked herself. Could she have stopped Myron? Had she wanted to?

Her own emotions were a mystery to her, and she found herself suddenly exhausted by all that had happened from the time she escaped to the stable till the moments in the kitchen when Josie had as much as told her that Myron was seriously interested in her.

Hearing her mother and Bob coming, Kerri hurried to her room, calling her "good night" over her shoulder so that she wouldn't have to face the questions she suspected her mother would have. If she couldn't understand her own feelings, how could she expect to explain them to anyone else?

As Kerri brushed her hair before going out to help set up for breakfast, she made a decision: She would have to talk to Derrick. She couldn't live with the idea that she'd hurt him. Just what she could say to him, however, was still beyond her.

Facing Sandy proved easier than expected. Her polite question, "Did the stains come out of your dress all right?" was met by a cold stare.

Finally, Sandy managed a smile. "The dress is fine. In fact, nothing happened that can't be repaired. I guess we'll both just have to be more careful from now on, won't we?"

"That's probably a good idea since we're working together," Kerri replied, taking the words as a sign of truce. "Are you serving on the cruise today?"

"Nope, I'm just going along to enjoy the ride," Sandy answered.

It seemed that breakfast was barely over when a hollow-sounding horn announced the approach of the *Lake Belle*. Kerri looked longingly toward the stable, but Derrick's horse wasn't tied to the hitch rail. The corrals were empty, as the horses had the day off to roam the pasture.

"Looking for someone?" Bob asked, pausing on his way to supervise the tying up of the boat.

"I just thought Derrick or LuAnn . . ." Kerri let it trail off.

"I doubt that they'll be coming," Bob said. "I think there's a rodeo in the area, and the Ridge Riders usually ride in the parade as a club unit." He frowned. "In fact, I think that was why Derrick was checking the assignment roster so carefully yesterday. He probably wanted to see if you'd be free to go."

"I was supposed to be free," she admitted, wondering if that was why Derrick was looking for her last night. "Only, I traded with Lucille so I'd have more days free after Donna gets here."

"Well, I—" He let it go as one of the guests called to him. "Talk to you later," he called over his shoulder.

Kerri turned back to the kitchen, wishing that she could change her mind. In spite of all the excitement last night, she no longer really wanted to go on the lake cruise.

"About time you put in an appearance," Myron called from the kitchen doorway. He grinned at her over the stack of boxes that had the muscles in his arms bulging with strain. "You're the one who's supposed to be working—I'm just helping out."

Kerri forced herself to smile and told him to hurry on down to the boat; then set herself to work, lending a hand with the packing of the food that they would be serving later. It seemed like a great deal of extra work, but as she joined the crowd going aboard, Kerri could hear the excitement in the guests' voices and she realized that it was probably worth it for them.

The *Lake Belle* was good-sized, with wide decks

dotted with benches and tables for the guests. The cabin was smaller and would be less comfortable if everyone was forced to crowd inside, Kerri thought. But then, on the lake there wouldn't be many times when people had to stay under cover until they reached a dock. The galley was compact but surprisingly efficient, and Mrs. O'Roarke obviously knew her way around it almost as well as she did around the lodge kitchen.

"Come up on deck as soon as you can, Kerri," Myron whispered as he came aboard with another load of supplies. "I'll point out all the local spots as we pass them."

"Historical monuments?" Kerri teased, aware of glares coming from Sandy, who was also helping in the galley—or at least taking up space there.

"More like the local lovers' lanes," Perry teased as he passed. "He'd know them all."

Everyone laughed, but Kerri could feel the blaze of color in her cheeks at the suggestion. So few of the boys she'd known in Spokane had had cars, but here almost everyone seemed to have one; and the way they talked . . .

"A pretty girl like Kerri won't have any trouble learning where all the best places are," Myron told everyone, his eyes caressing her face and sending shivers down her back. "City girls can always teach us country boys a thing or two." The words were almost a challenge.

"Please, I'm still trying to learn my way around the resort," Kerri stammered. It was definitely a new world here, she realized, and with the older boys like Myron . . .

Fortunately, Mrs. O'Roarke soon ordered everyone not assigned to work to get out of the kitchen. Kerri was able to relax a little as she followed the cook's instructions about storing the things the boys had carried aboard. By the time the *Lake Belle* tooted its intention of leaving, things were quite well organized.

"You girls can go up on deck for about an hour," Mrs. O'Roarke told her and Josie. "I won't need any help till it's time to start taking things up to the serving tables. Tell Les and Myron that I'll need them in about forty-five minutes."

"She sure has everything under control," Kerri observed as they climbed the short metal stairway to the glassed-in cabin. They stopped there, both looking all the way around the deck.

"I'll tell Les," Josie said. "You go join Myron."

Kerri opened her mouth to refuse, but Josie was already moving away from her. She stared after the older girl for a moment, wondering why their relationship seemed to have cooled. Was it just because Myron had expressed an interest in her? she asked herself. Could Josie be jealous?

Before she could think about it further, Myron turned around and, catching sight of her, signaled her to join him. Kerri hurried forward, trying to recapture the magic she knew she should be feeling at having been singled out to share the trip with him.

They stood on the deck of the boat, watching the handsome houses and resorts slide past. Myron seemed to know something amusing about each and every building, keeping her laughing even though she believed very little of what he told her. She was sorry when Les came by to remind Myron that he had to work as well as play on the trip.

"Are you free tonight, Kerri?" Myron asked before leaving her.

"Well . . . ah . . . yes, I guess so," Kerri gulped, caught between excitement and anxiety.

"Then how about coming into town with me after we get back? We can go to Dickerson's or The Rock Around for a while."

"Well, I . . . I have to ask Mom," Kerri murmured.

"I'll check with you after we get things set up for Mrs. O'Roarke," he told her, touching her lips with a light fingertip.

Kerri watched him go, then took a deep breath and made her way around the deck to where her mother was talking to some of the guests. As soon as she could catch her attention, she beckoned to her, waiting close to the cabin till her mother joined her.

"What is it, dear?" her mother asked. "Problem in the galley?"

"I just wondered if it would be all right if I went out with Myron after we get back," Kerri asked.

"Myron?" Her mother raised an eyebrow. "I thought that he and Sandy Kline were going together."

Kerri shrugged elaborately. "I don't think it was ever anything official. They just date each other between times." She tried to keep her tone light to hide the wild beating of her heart. "He offered to show me around a little more."

Her mother frowned, then shrugged. "I guess it will be all right, but don't be late, Kerri. We have another busy day tomorrow getting things ready for the next group of guests, and there is a ride in the afternoon and—" She stopped, looking guilty. "I guess I just wish you were going to be with Derrick," she finished.

"Oh Mom," Kerri protested.

"Okay, okay, I know. You're not a baby anymore." Her mother gave her shoulders a quick squeeze. "I just have to get used to having a grown-up daughter."

Kerri grinned. "Don't worry, Mom, I'll be home early. But now I have to go below and help Mrs. O'Roarke."

Kerri nearly bumped into a heavily laden Myron as she went down the stairway. "Whoa! Take it easy! Is it okay for tonight?" he asked, shifting the boxes.

Kerri nodded, thinking that, in the half-shadowy area of the boat he looked just like a Viking warrior. All he lacked was the golden beard. She remembered last night's kiss and shivered at the thought that he might kiss her again.

"We'll leave as soon as we get everything unloaded after the cruise, okay?" he asked.

"I'd like to change," Kerri said.

He shrugged. "You look cute now, but whatever you say."

Kerri blushed and plunged away from him, heading for the galley to see what Mrs. O'Roarke had for her to do. She was glad to be busy, since she really didn't want to think about the evening ahead.

It wasn't till much later, while she and Josie were clearing the last of the tables, that Josie asked, "Is it true?"

"Is what true?" Kerri asked, stopping for a moment to enjoy the cool breeze that was coming up as the afternoon drew to a close and the *Lake Belle* chugged toward the distant resort dock.

"Are you going out with Myron tonight?" Josie's green eyes, usually so clear, were unreadable.

Kerri nodded. "He asked me before lunch. How did you know?"

Josie sighed. "Sandy said he would ask you."

"Sandy?" Kerri felt a sharp sting of jealousy. "How did she know?"

Josie shrugged. "She just said she'd bet he would."

Kerri took a deep breath. "Do you think he just asked me out to make her jealous?" she asked, almost afraid to hear the answer.

Josie leaned against the table she'd been clearing and pushed at her brown hair, which the damp lake breeze had left straight and wispy. "Probably not," she answered. "If it was the other way around, I'd say yes. I think Sandy is furiously jealous and would like to make Myron unhappy, but where he's concerned . . . I think he just wants to take you out."

"I don't want to get between them," Kerri said, letting her breath out slowly. "I mean, even if I could compete with Sandy, I'd hate to try."

Josie laughed. "You've done pretty well so far, I'd say."

"Oh, I—"

"Come on, you two, we'll be docking before you get done," Bob called from the bow of the boat, ending the conversation.

Kerri moved to obey at once, but Josie's words stuck in her mind. Though she sensed that it hadn't exactly been meant as a compliment, she couldn't help but feel that it was. She was actually competing with Sandy Kline—little wallflower Kerri was actually dating someone like Myron Fuller, a graduated senior who made even Jamie Palmer look unimpressive.

She smiled to herself as she thought about the letter she'd been going to write to Donna, a letter confessing that she'd exaggerated a little where Myron was concerned. She wouldn't have to do that now, she told herself. After tonight it would all be true, she would be dating Myron.

8

Kerri had bought the orange sun dress in Spokane but had never had the occasion to wear it. She took it off the hanger carefully, savoring her happiness. The bodice had been a little large when she bought the dress, but now it fit just perfectly.

Her mother knocked, then came in as Kerri was brushing her hair, which was curly from the damp. She stopped in the doorway, frowning slightly.

"Don't you like it?" Kerri asked, her doubts surfacing at once.

"You look so grown up," her mother answered. "Different, I guess."

Kerri smiled. "I want to look older," she admitted. "I mean, Myron is eighteen."

"And you are just sixteen," her mother stated. "Don't forget that, Kerri. You don't have to keep up with him or with the girls in his crowd."

"Oh, Mom, I . . . We're just going into town to

Dickerson's to dance, that's all." Kerri tried to cover her own nervousness with irritation. "I'm not a little girl anymore."

Her mother's smile was tinged with sadness. "I wouldn't be worrying if you were," she replied, stepping forward to help Kerri fasten the slender gold chain with the single pearl that had been her gift on Kerri's sixteenth birthday.

Myron's expression changed as she stepped out onto the terrace where he'd been waiting, and Kerri felt a glow of satisfaction at the appreciation she could read in the usually unreadable gray eyes. "Sorry to keep you waiting," she told him.

"Worth every minute," he informed her. "I can see that I'm going to have to do better than old Dickerson's tonight."

"What do you mean?" Kerri asked as he held the door of his red Mustang for her.

"Well, I made a couple of phone calls while I was waiting, and it turns out that there is a lake party later on at Rocky Point. I thought we'd go into town and dance for a while, then pick up something to eat and finish the evening at the party. How does that sound to you?"

Kerri sneaked a sidelong glance at Myron's profile as he started the sporty little car and backed away from the lodge wall. "I did tell Mom we were going to Dickerson's," she managed, afraid to object to his plans, yet not sure that she wanted to go to the lake party. She hadn't heard much about them, just whispers among the older boys—whispers about beer busts and hangovers.

"And so we shall," Myron assured her with his most attractive grin. "We'll go there first."

Dickerson's was busy for a Sunday night, and Kerri was well aware of the envious stares from all the other girls the moment she entered. Being on Myron's arm was very different from entering with Derrick and LuAnn, she realized. Several younger boys vacated a front booth without hesitation, and everyone seemed to crowd around them the moment they were seated.

"Coke?" Myron asked Kerri

She nodded, breathless, feeling a little like a princess as everyone gathered around and asked her about working at the resort, living in Whitefish, what Spokane had been like. Myron seemed to take the adulation in his stride, hardly even noticing it as he went to get the drinks, then returned to ask her to dance.

Perhaps he really didn't notice it, Kerri thought as they danced. If he'd been treated that way all through high school, he probably didn't realize that no one else was. She giggled a little, remembering that someone had told her that Myron wasn't conceited, only convinced. Now she could see that the description was accurate.

"Having a good time?" Myron asked, smiling down at her.

"Oh, yes," Kerri answered with total honesty.

They stayed for only three more dances, finishing their Cokes in between; then Myron looked around with a bored gaze. "How about going on to The Rock Around?" he suggested. "We can get pizza and beer there, and the crowd is a little more lively."

Kerri felt a twinge of regret about leaving the familiar safety of Dickerson's, but she could see that Myron was impatient, and if she wanted him to continue asking her out . . .

She swallowed hard and forced a smile. "Ready when you are," she answered.

The Rock Around was outside of town on the road that led to Kalispell, the next town. It was a shabby building, but the parking lot surrounding it was full of cars. The beat of the music could be clearly heard long before they reached the psychedelically striped door.

"This is more like it," Myron said as they stepped inside. "Let's see if we can find someone willing to share a table."

Kerri had difficulty really seeing anything as a light-bar spun various colors and intensities of light through the smoky air and over the crowded booths and tables that ringed a large, crowded dance floor. Myron began waving almost at once and, taking her arm firmly, forced his way through the crowd till they reached the edge of the dance floor where Perry Snyder and a pretty blonde were beckoning.

"I knew I'd find somebody to share a table," Myron said, dropping into a chair. "The crowd here is harder to get through than a goal-line stand in the fourth quarter. What are we drinking, Perry?"

"Beer," Perry answered, and the blonde, whom he'd introduced as Denise, nodded.

"Kerri?" Myron asked.

"Just Coke for me," Kerri murmured.

"Nobody is checking IDs," Myron told her. "If you want beer with your pizza, it's okay."

For a moment she hesitated. She wanted to be more like the cool blonde, whose mocking eyes she could feel. But the smell of the half-empty glasses on the table told her that she'd hate the taste. "Just Coke for me, thanks, and pizza. I thought I'd never be hungry again after all that food we had on the boat, but suddenly I'm starving."

It wasn't exactly the truth, but it seemed to ease the moment, and after a brief discussion of what should be on the pizza, Myron vanished into the crowd once again. Kerri turned her attention to Perry, glad of a familiar face. "Where's Josie tonight?" she asked, more to make conversation than because she really wanted to know.

Perry shrugged. "She doesn't come here much."

Kerri tried to think of something else to say, but with the music so loud, it hardly seemed worth the effort. She tried smiling at Denise, but the blonde simply looked past her and sipped her beer.

Myron insisted on showing Kerri several new dance steps when they fought their way out onto the floor. He made no further mention of her refusal to drink with him, getting her a second Coke when she finished her first one.

If it hadn't been for Denise, she would have enjoyed herself; but as soon as Myron returned to the table the first time, Kerri understood the blonde's coldness. Denise was all shiny white teeth and batting false eyelashes whenever Myron looked her way, and Kerri could see Perry wasn't happy about it.

After about an hour of watching, Perry's blue eyes were angry and he wasn't smiling when he asked Kerri to dance—after Denise had neatly wrangled an invitation from Myron. Kerri tried in vain to think of something funny or clever to say.

"I'm sorry if Denise is spoiling your evning," Perry said, breaking the silence between them. "She's a tourist I met night before last at Dickerson's."

Kerri shrugged. "We're going to have to leave pretty soon, anyway. I promised Mom that I'd be home fairly early."

"You aren't going out to the lake party?" Perry sounded surprised.

Kerri squinted at her watch in the ever-changing light. "It's almost midnight."

"That's when the parties get going good," Perry told her. "I think I'll take Denise up there for a while—if she can tear herself away from Myron."

Kerri studied Perry, surprised to hear very little anger in his voice when he mentioned Myron's name. She wondered if she would have been as understanding if Myron had responded more enthusiastically to Denise's flirting. Somehow she doubted it.

As soon as the four of them returned to the table, Perry announced that he and Denise were going to leave for the lake party.

"As a matter of fact, that's just what I had in mind," Myron said before Kerri could say a word. "What about it, honey?" He looked her way expectantly.

Kerri opened her mouth to say that she couldn't, but the words wouldn't come out, not while Denise's eyes were on her. "I . . . ah . . . haven't finished my Coke," she murmured, hating herself for a coward.

"You guys go on ahead," Myron told Perry. "We'll be along a little later. I'd like one more dance with my lady here."

The words were like music to her ears, and Kerri found it easy to ignore the worries she'd felt before. His lady! It was magic. It made her special in a way she'd never felt before. She coaxed him into staying for several dances, but finally her glass was empty and she could think of no more excuses.

As she followed Myron through the crowd and out into the parking lot, Kerri checked her watch again. It was nearly half-past-twelve. "Myron," she said, slowing him before they reached the car.

"What is it Kerri?" he asked.

"I think we've got a problem about the lake party," she began, choosing her words carefully, hoping and praying that she could make him understand—so that he wouldn't think she was too much of a child and never ask her out again.

"Don't you want to go?" he asked, then grinned. "Even if I promise that we'll spread our blanket on the side of the bonfire away from Denise?"

Kerri giggled. "I think she'd move," she observed. "But she's not the reason. It's just the time. I promised Mom that I wouldn't be late, and it's already after midnight."

"Oh, come on. One o'clock isn't that late," he protested. "We don't have to stay that long, but we should put in an appearance." His grin deepened. "Give you a chance to tell everyone that you've been to a real lake party."

"Well, I'd love to, but—"

"Come on, Kerri, it's not that far from the ranch. We've got time for one beer with the gang, then I swear I'll take you home. Isn't that fair?" His expression had changed slightly, though his tone was still light and teasing. She could see the challenge in his eyes, and she had the icy feeling that if she didn't accept, she'd never have another chance with him.

"Well, maybe a little while," she murmured, "but I don't want to get in trouble now. I mean, I just can't be grounded while Donna is here."

He laughed, putting an arm around her as they neared the car. "Heck no, we just might want to take Donna to a lake party sometime."

A double date, with one of Myron's friends taking Donna—It would undoubtedly be the high point of Donna's stay at the lodge. She would just have to make her mother understand, she decided; somehow she'd have to make it right.

The drive along the lake was heavenly as she sat close to Myron's side, his arm around her shoulders. She felt a twinge of conscience as they drove past the turnoff that led to the lodge, but a slight squeeze from Myron's arm banished her doubts. He was so handsome and exciting. . . .

Kerri thought about Denise and the way she'd flirted with him, and enjoyed the knowledge that the older girl would have done anything to trade places with her.

The road seemed to disappear suddenly, and Myron needed both hands on the wheel as the Mustang bounced down an overgrown trail that meandered between the pines. Kerri sat forward, peering into the darkness, her doubts and anxieties reviving.

When Myron finally stopped, Kerri's heart sank. It was just as she'd feared. The small meadow was protected on all sides by the towering pines, and they dwarfed the low-burning campfire in the middle. In the silence that followed the killing of the car motor, she could hear the soft sounds of a transistor radio and low giggles.

"Come on," Myron said. "Grab a beer out of the ice chest behind the seat and let's go see what's happening."

"I really don't want anything to drink," Kerri managed to say as she slid out of the car and looked around. Several of the couples nearer the soft light of

the fire waved and called greetings to Myron, but
many of the dim shapes beyond seemed oblivious.

"Come on, Kerri." Myron's arm slipped around her
waist; his hand, cold from the ice chest, sent shivers
down her spine.

Kerri moved beside him, feeling as though she were
being led to trial. Even recognizing a few of the faces
around the fire didn't help, and she was terribly
conscious of those she really couldn't see in the
shadows. She'd heard of parties like this. There were
always stories about them in Spokane, about the
things the wilder crowd did; but to actually be
here . . .

"Well, well, look who is playing with the big kids."
Sandy's tone was mocking. Kerri jumped. Then she
spotted Sandy sitting on a blanket on the far side of
the fire.

"We just stopped by to see what's going on,"
Myron answered while Kerri was still trying to think
up a suitably cutting reply. "Looks to me like the
party is pretty quiet."

"That's not exactly bad," Sandy's date observed,
pulling Sandy closer to his side. "I like it better than a
noisy brawl."

Myron spread the blanket he'd been carrying on a
little ridge of grass and eased Kerri down beside him,
holding her close as he opened the beer can and took
a long swallow. "Sure you won't have a sip?" he
asked.

Kerri shook her head, fighting tears. Everything
had been so wonderful before, but now . . . Myron
had had three or four glasses of beer at The Rock
Around, and now he was drinking more. Would that
make him different? She was suddenly afraid of the

vast emptiness of the woods and the lake beyond. She found herself shivering again, though not from the cold.

"Hey, I'd better warm you up," Myron said before he kissed her.

Kerri tried to relax, but her shivers increased and, to her horror, her teeth began to chatter as though it were twenty below instead of merely a cool early summer night.

Myron released her lips and drew away. "Kerri, are you all right?" he asked.

"I . . . I don't know," she whispered. "I feel kind of strange, Myron. Like maybe I was too warm in The Rock Around and now I'm so cold. . . . I think I'd better go home."

For a moment she could see anger flaring in his eyes; then another spasm of shivers shook her, and his anger changed to concern. He wrapped the blanket around her shoulder and stood up, then bent to pick her up as though she weighed no more than a feather.

Several of the young people called teasing remarks after them, but Kerri couldn't even hear them clearly. She found it wonderfully comforting to snuggle against Myron's chest as he carried her to the car. By the time he'd set her inside, her shivering had almost stopped.

"Are you going to be all right?" he asked as he slid in under the wheel.

"I think so," Kerri replied. "I guess I'll just have to learn to dress warmer here at night."

"Next time bring a sweater," he advised, starting the car.

Kerri leaned back against the seat with a sigh of contentment. *Next time.* The words were reassuring.

"I'm sorry about ruining your time at the party," she murmured as they drove back through the night.

He shrugged. "There will be plenty more parties this summer. We'll just arrange to get to the next one earlier."

The promise of those words and the memory of Myron's gentle concern as he'd carried her to the car kept Kerri from thinking of anything else till they reached the lodge. Only as Myron slowed to park did she realize that all the lights were still burning inside and outside the building.

Bob and her mother were on the front porch even before the car stopped. "Oh no," Kerri groaned, suddenly aware of the time. "They'll kill me."

"Let me do the talking," Myron whispered. "Just follow my lead." He was out of the car before she could protest.

"Mr. Harriman, Mrs. Harriman, I hope you haven't been worrying about Kerri," he began even as she slipped the blanket off her shoulders and got out of the car.

"Where have you been, Myron?" Bob asked, his face stern.

"Would you believe we had a flat, and my spare was flat too when I put it on? I had to wait till someone came by and I could borrow a tire. I was just lucky that I could get one that fit."

"I'm awfully sorry, Mom, Bob," Kerri murmured, coming to stand beside Myron. "I would have called to tell you, but there was no phone around by the time it got late enough that you'd be worrying." Though she was speaking the strict truth herself, Kerri could feel the guilty weight of Myron's lie. "I really feel terrible about worrying both of you."

"Well, at least you're home safely," her mother said.

"And I've learned a good lesson," Myron continued. "From now on when I put air in my tires, I'll check the spare as well. I promise it will never happen again, Mrs. Harriman. Kerri told me that she had to be home early, and we left town in plenty of time, but . . . I do hope you'll forgive me."

In spite of her feelings of shame and guilty embarrassment, Kerri had to fight down an urge to giggle at the expression on Myron's face. He was so convincing, she could almost see them on the road: the flat tire, the sinking spare. She couldn't help wondering how many times he'd used the excuse before; he did it so well.

"Just don't you be late tomorrow morning," Bob told him.

Myron reached out and gently caressed Kerri's cheek. "See you in the morning," he told her as their eyes met with an intimacy that was almost like a kiss.

"Thanks for everything," Kerri called after him, then shivered as the cold night air touched her again.

"Are you all right?" her mother asked, coming to put an arm around her.

"I'm just not used to the way it cools off here at night," Kerri answered, keeping her head down so that she wouldn't have to meet her mother's eyes. Now that Myron was gone, the shame of the lie came back. She wished that she'd insisted on telling the truth. Even being grounded would be better than feeling so guilty. Besides, it wasn't as though she'd done anything to be ashamed of. It was just that time had slipped by too fast and . . .

"You go right to bed," her mother said, interrupting her thoughts. "We can discuss this in the morning. I don't want you getting sick."

Kerri accepted the reprieve gladly, heading for her room as fast as she could. She was sure that she'd never be able to sleep after all that had happened. She longed to be alone in the safety of her bed to remember each wonderful moment.

9

Kerri woke from a confusing and unhappy dream with a feeling that the day ahead was going to be unpleasant. A glance at the window seemed to confirm her suspicions, for the sky was as gray as her feelings.

The rain began even before they'd finished serving breakfast, and the morning was madness. Trying to keep the guests amused, they continued the normal work of cleaning and of preparing for the next meal. It was nearly noon before Kerri realized that she hadn't seen Myron during any of her trips through the lobby and dining room of the lodge.

"Perry," she called as the tall, dark-haired boy crossed the lobby.

"Hi, Kerri," he said, coming over and smothering a yawn. "How are you surviving?"

She shrugged. "Okay, I guess. How about you? Did you have a good time last night?"

"That's something you should ask Myron about, not me." Perry's expression was less than friendly.

"I haven't seen him around so far today," Kerri admitted. "Besides, what would he know about your evening?"

"He's probably sleeping in the stable or the equipment shed," Perry snapped. "I doubt that he got in before dawn."

"But he brought me home as soon as we left the party," Kerri protested. A sudden suspicion crept into her mind. "He didn't go back, did he?"

Perry nodded. "Last I saw of him was when I left about two. He and Denise were dancing."

"Denise." Kerri swallowed hard, feeling somehow ashamed, as though it might be her fault.

"I'd like to bash him for it," Perry said, "but it isn't even his fault. He doesn't do a thing to attract them. He came out to have a beer with some of the guys. She went to him."

Kerri tried to think of something to say, but no words came. One of the guests called her over, asking for more coffee. Perry went on his way with a weary wave.

As she worked, Kerri tried to sort out her feelings about Myron. Was she jealous? There was a twinge of it as she pictured Myron kissing the sultry-eyed Denise, but more than that, she felt something like disappointment. Hadn't their date been enough for him? Was she too boring and unsophisticated for him? She closed her eyes, momentarily picturing herself and Myron as one of the couples wrapped in each other's arms in the meadow. Her shivers returned, and she knew that they had nothing to do with the coolness of the rainy day.

After lunch, she went to the resort office to find Bob so she could ask him about Derrick.

"Oh, he won't be over today, honey," Bob replied. "I called him right after breakfast and told him not to bother bringing the horses in today."

"Oh." Kerri swallowed her disappointment and started to turn away.

"Have you got a problem, Kerri?" Bob asked, getting up and closing the office door before she could leave. "You didn't have any trouble with young Fuller, did you? He's got a reputation for being quite the playboy."

"Oh no, he didn't do anything," Kerri assured him, feeling the weight of the lie that Myron had told last night. "Really, we just danced and ate pizza."

"And went up to the lake party at Rocky Point." His tone was light, but his dark eyes met hers levelly. "I used a variation of the flat-tire story on the parents of my girl friends when I was Myron's age," he continued.

Kerri felt the red burning in her cheeks, and she dropped her gaze so he wouldn't see the tears that filled her eyes. "I . . . I didn't know he was going to lie. We only stayed a few minutes at the party. I . . . I got so cold and—" She stopped. "Does Mom know?" she asked.

He shook his head. "I think you should tell her, though, Kerri."

"She won't let me date Myron again."

"Would that be so awful?"

Kerri considered for a moment. "He really was nice, Bob, and I do like him a lot."

"More than Derrick?"

Kerri could only shrug.

"Tell you what," Bob said. "You tell your mother

the truth and I'll go find Myron and have a little talk with him."

"You won't fire him?" Kerri gasped.

Bob laughed gently. "Of course not," he assured her. "I just want to let him know that he can't lie to me." He gave her shoulders a little pat. "Don't worry. I'm not going to do a heavy father number. You're old enough to be responsible. I just want to keep things honest around here. I don't want any lies messing up a good summer." He lifted her head till their eyes met. "Okay?"

Kerri nodded. She felt better now that the truth was out.

"Shall I ask your mother to come in here now?" he asked.

"I guess I might as well get it over with," Kerri agreed.

It was easier than she'd expected, though the hurt in her mother's face made her feel guilty all over again. Once she'd told her everything, her mother sighed. "He really is too old for you, Kerri," she observed. "Not just in age, but in experience. A party like that is no place for you."

"But nothing happened," Kerri protested. "He brought me right home when I asked him to."

"And then lied to us."

Kerri looked down at her hand. "Please don't say I can't date him again," she pleaded. "I mean, he might not ever ask me out again, but if he does . . . if I promise not to go to Rocky Point with him, couldn't I . . ." She let it trail off, sneaking a glance at her mother through the thick veil of her eyelashes.

Her mother sighed. "I think it would be just as well if you don't date anyone till Donna gets here," she said. "There are plenty of activities here on the ranch to keep you busy, and that will give you a little time to think things over."

"You mean I'm grounded?" Kerri wailed.

Her mother's eyes met hers firmly. "Well, you were an hour late getting home last night, Kerri. And it is just ten days till Donna arrives."

"Myron will think I'm a child," she protested, but without heat.

"He'll think that you have parents who care about where you are and what you do, that's all. And he'll know that he can't play games with the truth where you're concerned. I think that's something important, too, don't you?"

Kerri nodded.

Her mother hugged her. "I'm proud of you, honey," she whispered, smoothing down Kerri's wildly curling hair. "It took courage to tell me about last night, and I think I'll feel a lot better about your dating from now on."

"In ten days," Kerri replied mournfully. Then their eyes met, and she found herself giggling with her mother.

"From the looks of things, we're going to be so busy for the next ten days, you'll probably be too tired to care," her mother told her. "Besides, if I remember correctly, you've traded with everyone, so you'll be working morning, noon and night."

"My mother, the slave driver," Kerri teased just as a tap on the door interrupted them.

Josie opened the door and put her head in. "Mrs. Harriman, one of the guests is asking about poker chips," she said. "Do we have any?"

"I'd better get out to the kitchen," Kerri murmured, suddenly conscious of the tearstains on her cheeks. "When the guests can't go out, they all like to eat."

When she reached the kitchen, she found Myron waiting for her, his pale hair sparkling with rain, his gray eyes bright. "You okay?" he asked.

"I'll survive," Kerri replied coolly, remembering what Perry had told her. "Did you have a nice time at the party?"

Myron's easy smile faltered a little, then became rueful. "News travels fast, doesn't it?" he asked.

He seemed to expect her to say something, but Kerri couldn't find words to express what she was feeling. She moved to the sink and rinsed her hands, wiping her face with the cool water at the same time. After a few minutes, Myron cleared his throat and sighed.

"I'm sorry about getting you into trouble last night," he said. "It was a dumb lie and I should have known Mr. Harriman would see through it. Was your Mom really mad?"

"They talked about shooting me at sunrise, but since it rained—" The joking words fell flat, but Kerri couldn't bring herself to tell him that she'd been grounded. It made her sound like such a child, and she was already unsure enough of him.

"I'll make it up to you," Myron told her, moving toward the door to the dining room, "but right now I've got a list of chores a mile long. Your stepfather has his own ideas of revenge."

Kerri watched him go, feeling a little let down but relieved, too. At least they were still friends, she told herself, and he had said that he'd make it up to her—whatever that meant. Standing alone in the kitchen brought other memories to mind, and her

smile faded. There was still one person left that she
needed to talk to. Tomorrow morning, she simply had
to try to explain things to Derrick—somehow.

Fortunately for everyone's good temper, the storm
blew itself away by early evening, and Tuesday
dawned sunny and new-washed. Kerri hurried
through her morning chores, grateful that many of the
guests had left and that the new ones had not yet
arrived—so that she could finish up early and have an
hour free before she had to help with the preparations
for lunch.

The moment she could leave, she headed for the
corrals where LuAnn and Derrick were busy sorting
out and cleaning up the horses for the day's ride.
LuAnn saw her first and waved happily. Derrick said
nothing, though he looked up when Kerri called a
greeting.

"What can we do for you?" LuAnn asked. "Are
you going to be free to go on the ride with us today?"

Kerri shook her head. "I'm afraid not. I don't get
out till Friday. I just thought I'd come down and see if
I could help. I know there's a lot to be done with all
the horses being muddy and everything." Her offer
sounded a little flat even to her own ears, and
Derrick's obvious lack of enthusiasm made her feel
foolish.

"Hey, that's great," LuAnn said. "They really are a
mess. You'd think the rain would wash them clean,
but I swear every one we want to use today has rolled
in the mud and has to be washed as well as groomed.
Here, we can start with these two." She handed Kerri
the leadrope from a bay, then led the way around the
stable to where a hose with a spray attachment
waited.

Kerri cast a couple of glances back toward the

corrals, but Derrick showed no sign of following them; so she had little choice but to help LuAnn with the washing, which the horses seemed to enjoy. "Did you have a good weekend?" she asked after a few minutes.

"Terrific. We went to the rodeo over at Silver Falls." LuAnn paused, and Kerri felt her eyes on her. "I was sort of hoping that you'd come with us," she went on, "but Derrick said you were busy."

"Busy." Kerri swallowed hard. "I had to work the boat cruise Sunday. I guess he saw my name on the list. I'm really sorry to have missed the rodeo. I've never been to one, so . . ."

"You'd love it," LuAnn assured her, then launched into a description of all that had happened, leaving Kerri free to feel miserable. Her name hadn't been on the cruise list, and she knew only too well why Derrick had said she was busy.

"I hear you dated God's gift to the girls," LuAnn said, interrupting her thoughts violently.

"What?" Kerri gasped.

LuAnn grinned at her. "I sort of expected you to be followed by a little pink cloud or something," she teased. "Or didn't you like Myron as well as you thought you would?"

"Who told you we went out?" Kerri asked instead of answering LuAnn's question.

"At least three people," LuAnn answered. "You can't do anything in Whitefish without everybody knowing." She giggled. "Are you going to tell me about it?"

"Well, it was great," Kerri admitted reluctantly, sure that LuAnn would tell Derrick everything she said. "We went to Dickerson's for a while, then to a place called The Rock Around for pizza."

"How about the lake party?" LuAnn asked. "Did he take you there?"

"Just for a few minutes," Kerri murmured, remembering what Perry had told her, and sure that story would be going the rounds too. "It was getting late and I'd promised Mom that I'd be home early."

"Snooty Sandy must have turned bright green," LuAnn observed with a rather malicious giggle.

"She was there with someone else," Kerri said quietly.

LuAnn shook her head. "It doesn't mean a thing. Everybody knows that she only dates other guys to keep Myron in line. I guess she wasn't counting on you, though. I mean, he always dates some of the tourist girls in the summer, but you'll be here all summer and in the fall, too." The light of gossip faded from her eyes and she became serious. "Do you really like him, Kerri?" she asked.

Kerri met her direct gaze, then looked away. "I don't know," she admitted. "It was fun and he was really nice, but . . . I guess it just didn't seem real, if you know what I mean."

LuAnn rolled her eyes. "No date with Myron Fuller could be anything but a dream," she observed. "Did you—" She stopped.

Kerri looked around and saw that Derrick had come around the corner of the stable, leading two more horses. "You trying to scrub the spots off the pinto?" he asked sharply.

"We're through," LuAnn answered, taking the leadrope from Kerri's nerveless fingers. "I'll take these two around and tie them. Kerri can help you with those two." She was gone before Kerri could object.

Derrick handed Kerri the leadropes without a

word. She searched her mind for something to say as she looked at his rather stern profile. Obviously, it wasn't going to be as easy as she'd hoped.

"Get a tight hold on the gray," Derrick ordered, breaking the silence. "She's kind of skittish and she's liable to step on you if you aren't watching."

Kerri had her hands full for several minutes and was glad for the distraction. By the time the mare was finished, she was feeling a little more in control of herself. "LuAnn was telling me what a great time you had at the rodeo," she began.

Derrick lifted his head, and their eyes met for the first time. The look was long and intense, but Kerri found herself unable to read it clearly. Her eyes were the first to drop, and she knew at once that there was nothing she could say to Derrick that would change what he'd seen when he entered the kitchen Saturday night. She'd been kissing Myron and she'd gone out with him last night.

"It was a good rodeo," Derrick said, his eyes now on the second horse as he began washing the mud off its back and legs.

"LuAnn said that one of the girls from the Ridge Riders placed in barrel racing," Kerri went on, wishing now that she hadn't come seeking Derrick's company. "I was just going to ask her what that is."

"It's kind of hard to explain," Derrick answered, "but if you'd like to see someone do it, you could come to practice with us Wednesday night. LuAnn has a colt she's training for barrel racing at the club arena. He stopped spraying water on the horse and looked at her. "Would you like to go, Kerri?"

"Oh, I'd love to," Kerri began, then she remembered her mother's punishment. "I can't," she said. "Not this week or next, I—"

"That's okay. It was just an idea." Derrick turned away, his shoulders stiff as he finished the second horse. "You can take them around and tie them with the others," he told her, not even looking her way. "They're the last that we'll need today."

His tone was a dismissal, leaving her nothing to do but walk away with the horses. There was no way she could explain about being grounded, not without telling him all about her date with Myron. And she couldn't do that.

The feeling of failure stayed with her after she tied the two horses to the corral rail with the others, and aware that there was nothing she could say or do now, she glanced at her watch. "I guess I'd better get back to the lodge," she told LuAnn. "Time to start setting up for lunch."

"See you later," LuAnn called. "Thanks for helping."

Kerri nodded, but her smile held no happiness. She felt strangely lonely and out of place as she trudged back across the grass to the terrace. What was the matter with her? she asked herself bitterly. What did she care if Derrick was mad at her?

With the resort now filled to capacity, there was more work for everyone and very little free time. By evening each night, Kerri was perfectly happy to stay in the lobby with her mother and Bob till the guests said good night.

She was torn between dreading and looking forward to Friday afternoon, when it would be her turn to go on the ride. She had seen almost nothing of Derrick since their brief encounter Tuesday morning. He and LuAnn came over only for the rides, and left right afterwards.

When she went out to the kitchen Friday morning, Bob was waiting for her, a cup of coffee resting on the counter as he nibbled at a bacon-and-egg sandwich, his favorite breakfast. "What's up?" Kerri asked, helping herself to a piece of toast before she started work.

"I was just wondering if you wanted to change your mind about today's ride," he said.

"Why?" Kerri turned to face him. "Did Derrick say something about not wanting me to go?"

"Derrick?" Bob frowned. "Heavens no, why should he?"

Kerri blushed. "I think he's kind of unhappy with me because I went out with Myron," she confessed, wondering why she found it so easy to tell Bob such things when she couldn't talk to anyone else.

Bob laughed. "Jealous is probably a better word," he told her. "I think Derrick was pretty taken with you, Kerri. He really hasn't dated a lot, as far as I know, and you have to admit Myron Fuller is about the stiffest competition a guy could have."

"I don't see why I can't date both of them," Kerri murmured. Then, remembering what he'd said, asked, "Why don't you want me to go on today's ride?"

"It's a long one, that's all," Bob answered. "I just thought you might still be a little soft for it. You haven't had much chance to ride since you've been here."

"Actually, I've been riding almost every afternoon," Kerri said crossly.

"I didn't know that." Bob frowned.

"I've been taking Sky Writer out for short rides." "She's so gentle I've been riding her bareback. I'll be all right today."

"I won't worry about you, then, although I wish you'd take a different horse, Kerri. I know you like Sky Writer and you haven't had any trouble with her, but I keep remembering LuAnn last year. She was crazy about that mare, too. And it was on the Bear Meadows ride that she had trouble with her."

"Is today's ride to Bear Meadows?" Kerri asked.

Bob shook his head. "That would be an all-day ride. Today you just go as far as the ridge turnoff, then head back down a shorter return trail. Bear Meadows is kind of a rough climb after you make the turn."

"Are there really bears up there?" Kerri asked, more to keep Bob distracted so he wouldn't forbid her to ride Sky Writer than because she really wanted to know.

"I haven't heard of anybody seeing any recently, but I can tell you there was a bear up there six or seven years ago, that's for sure."

"What happened?" Kerri's curiosity was aroused.

"It darn near killed one of my mares. The whole herd was in the area, and this mare had evidently left the others to have her foal. Anyway, Derrick's dad and I were out checking the horses when we heard the mare squealing and knew she was in trouble. We headed in her direction and got there just in time to get a couple of shots at the bear before it disappeared into the brush."

"Did you kill it?" Kerri gasped. Her mind filled with pictures that were like something out of a movie.

Bob shook his head. "Didn't even hit it, as far as we could tell. Anyway, we didn't have time to mess with the bear. We had to get the mare down to the road and into a horse trailer so we could get her to a vet."

Kerri felt sick. "Was she badly hurt?" she asked fearfully.

"She'd been clawed quite a bit and needed a lot of stitching up, but she had kept the bear from killing her foal. The filly had a couple of scratches on its side and a big notch of hide and hair torn out of its neck, but it was okay. The mare was too sick to feed the foal, though, so the vet kept it and hand-raised it. I didn't have the time or the patience."

"Did anyone ever get the bear?"

"I don't think so. A couple of hunting parties tried tracking it, but that's real rough country beyond the meadows. The bear probably headed for Canada after it left us. Anyway, that's how Bear Meadows got their name."

"That's some story," Kerri told him, then turned her attention to getting down the glasses that were to be filled with juice. As she'd hoped, he made a couple more comments about the trails, then left the kitchen to attend to his own morning duties, totally forgetting his earlier doubts about her riding Sky Writer.

The ride left immediately after lunch, so Kerri was excused from clearing the tables and the usual cleanup chores. She hurried to her room to change from her work clothes to her older Levi's, boots—and a long-sleeved shirt that would protect her from the scratching branches of the heavy pines that sometimes grew out into the trails. She was very surprised when Myron followed her from the terrace toward the stable and corrals.

"Are you assigned to this ride, too?" she asked.

"I traded Les," Myron answered. "Long ride, more staff riders." He grinned at her. "I saw your name on the list."

Kerri felt a glow of pleasure burning in her cheeks, but no words came, and she was relieved to have LuAnn call for help with a tall brown gelding who was proving hard to catch as he ducked behind the other horses in the corral. "Talk to you later," she told Myron and slipped between the corral bars, moving to cut the gelding off so he couldn't escape to the far side of the corral. The horse surrendered amiably.

"You're a lazy bum, Sparky," LuAnn told the gelding as she snapped the leadrope on his halter, then rubbed his neck. "Unfortunately, you're also a terrific trail horse, so you have to work."

"What other horses do you need?" Kerri asked, checking the lineup at the rail with an experienced eye.

"The sorrel mare, the gray, and whatever horses you and Myron want to ride," was the quick answer.

"I want Sky Writer," Kerri replied. "Myron, what horse do you want?" She picked up the leadropes that were looped around the corral post. Sky Writer was already nuzzling her arm, and the sorrel was easy to catch, so she took them out first, tying them with the rest.

"How is the big bay?" Myron asked, addressing LuAnn.

"He's got a hard mouth, but he's not bad to ride," she answered. "Want him?"

Myron nodded. "I'll get him," he said as LuAnn brought out the gray.

"Where's Derrick?" Kerri asked as she picked up a brush and began helping LuAnn clean the corral dust from the backs and necks of the tied horses.

"One of the horses had a loose shoe, so he and Mr. Harriman are working on it in the stable," LuAnn answered. "That's why we're running late with the saddling."

"You tell me what saddle goes on what horse and I'll give you a hand," Myron offered. "We're going to have guests underfoot in about twenty minutes, so we'd better get moving."

"I'll clean them, you dress them," Kerri said, handing him the leadropes for the two horses she'd brushed down.

Myron chuckled. "You pick the outfits, LuAnn," he instructed, "and I'll put them on the horses."

LuAnn led the way to the stable, giggling. Kerri felt better about the day. Whatever mood Derrick was in, at least she and LuAnn and Myron could laugh.

Myron's warning about the arrival of the guests turned out to be only too accurate. Some were leaning on the fence and asking questions even before she'd finished grooming the last horse. LuAnn and Myron, Bob and Derrick, were all at work in the stable bridling and saddling the horses as fast as possible, but they still had difficulty sorting everyone out and getting them mounted on the proper horses.

Kerri saddled Sky Writer herself, feeling Derrick's disapproving stare even as she worked. Fortunately, he had no time to offer any criticisms before he had to take his place at the head of the line. Between them, he and LuAnn sorted the riders into a relatively neat line, spacing Myron and Kerri carefully between groups of guests. Then they were on their way, leaving a waving Bob behind them.

10

Though Kerri would have preferred to ride with Derrick, Myron or LuAnn, she knew that she was responsible for the guests. She did her best to answer their questions and to keep an eye on them and their mounts. The trail was a nice one, wide enough for easy riding, yet rising and falling over ridges that offered breathtaking views of the mountains and the lake.

At first Kerri noticed no change in Sky Writer, but as the trail wound higher and farther from the lakeshore, she sensed something different about the mare. Though the day was cool, the black-and-white shoulders were damp to her touch, and she could feel the tension of the muscles under the silky hide. She no longer just walked, her steps were choppy. At other times, she danced along, pulling at the bit as though she wanted to run.

Kerri tried talking to her, patting at the same time, but it did no good. When they stopped near a fork in the trail, she rode back to the end of the line where LuAnn was riding. "Could we trade places for a while?" she asked, hating to meet the girl's gaze.

LuAnn looked at the mare and shook her head. "You can go back to the resort if you want," she said. "This is a pretty fair bunch of riders. Myron, Derrick and I can handle them."

"No. It's okay. It's just that Sky Writer's a little jittery and I don't want to risk making the other horses nervous. We'll be fine back here."

LuAnn's eyes offered sympathy, but she said nothing, just nodded and rode forward. Sky Writer danced in place, her black tail switching as though she were besieged by flies, though there were none in the clear air. "Don't do this to me, horse," Kerri whispered. "I don't want you to have to be sold, but if you do something dumb . . ."

The mare tossed her head, fighting the bit and Kerri's firm hold, her small hooves restless on the pine-needle-coated trail. Luckily, Derrick began moving forward again, passing the trail that headed up into the higher country and turning down a shady pathway that seemed to angle back toward the lake.

Sky Writer pranced along for about half a mile, then as suddenly as it had begun, the mood seemed to pass and she settled down. Her coat dried, and Kerri slowly relaxed in the saddle, once more secure in her feeling that she could trust the mare.

When Derrick stopped again, Kerri rode forward. "She's okay now," she told LuAnn. "She never really did anything, but . . ."

LuAnn nodded. "That's the way she was with me,

Kerri, only she kept getting worse and worse. By the time we got to the meadows, she was crazier than some spoiled racehorse."

"She quieted down after I started riding drag," Kerri went on. "Maybe she was just feeling crowded or something."

"Maybe." LuAnn's tone held little confidence. "Want to try her in the line the rest of the way?"

"Might as well," Kerri answered. "She seems to be fine now."

The rest of the ride was uneventful, but Kerri couldn't shake the feeling of depression that had come with Sky Writer's first change of mood. No matter what she'd said to LuAnn when they switched places, the mare had changed. The horse she'd ridden up on the high trail had been frighteningly different from the gentle, sweet-tempered creature who nuzzled her knee as they finished the ride.

The scents of barbecuing meat filled the air as Kerri helped with the unsaddling, but she was too worried about Sky Writer to be hungry. Still, she was very conscious of being alone in the stable with Derrick while LuAnn took the horses out to the corral.

"Are you coming to eat?" she asked softly. "There's the dance afterward."

Derrick looked at her over the back of the gray he'd been brushing, his brown eyes unreadable. "I don't know if LuAnn wants to," he observed.

"Do you want to?" Kerri asked.

"Do you want me to?" The words were spoken softly, without emphasis, but Kerri sensed their importance.

"Of course I do," she said. "I . . . I've missed you this past week."

"You've been busy." His tone was bitter.

"I've been working hard, trading everybody so that I'll have some free days when Donna gets here next week," Kerri continued, ignoring his tone. "It's kind of rough not having any time off now, but I know I'll be glad later."

"No time to play?"

"Only in the line of duty, like tonight," Kerri answered, meeting his gaze firmly. "So, are you coming?"

The slow smile melted his features and eased the coldness she'd been feeling all week. "I sure am hungry," he said. "I'd probably die of malnutrition before LuAnn and I could make the long ride home."

Kerri smiled at him, her heart light once again. "I've got to go change and help serve, but I'll see you later, so save me some dances."

"All you want." The words followed her as she led Sky Writer out of the stable into the late afternoon sunshine. She left the mare in the corral and hurried across the lawn to the lodge.

"You're late," her mother greeted her at the door. "You won't have time for a long bath, I'm afraid."

"I'll shower," Kerri assured her, heading for her room.

"You've got a letter waiting," her mother called after her. "Came just after you left."

Kerri picked up the envelope, noting that it was Donna's familiar handwriting. She opened it quickly, then dropped on the bed to read it, kitchen duties forgotten. The note was short.

"Dear Kerri," it began . . .

My folks just got a chance to take a trip to Mexico with the company Daddy works for.

They have to leave on Tuesday, which means they want me to leave Tuesday also.

Would it be terribly inconvenient if I arrived Tuesday instead of Thursday? Please, please let me know as soon as possible.

Love,
Donna.

P.S. I'm dying to meet Myron and to hear all the gory details of your dates with him. I'm positively green.

A tap on the door drew her attention away from the letter. Kerri looked up to see her mother standing in the doorway. "Kerri, we're going to need some help out here," she said.

Kerri handed her the letter and headed for her bathroom, pulling off her clothes as she turned on the shower. When she returned, her mother had taken her place on the bed.

"Can I call her and tell her it's okay?" Kerri asked. "I know I'm supposed to be grounded for ten days, but . . ."

"Of course it's okay, Kerri," her mother said. "We'll just say you've got time off for good behavior, all right? You can call her as soon as you finish cleaning up after dinner. I'll tell Bob. Now get dressed and get out there before the serving line is attacked by starving guests."

There was time for a quick hug before her mother left. Kerri hastily pulled on the orange-and-brown plaid peasant dress, her favorite among the ones her mother had made her. Her hair took a little taming, and with the addition of lipstick, she was as ready as she'd ever be. She hurried out to help carry the food from the kitchen to the serving table and took her place between Josie and Sandy. It was going to be a busy evening, she was sure.

The serving went quickly, as Kerri told Josie about Donna's letter. LuAnn and Derrick appeared about midway through the line of people, and Kerri gave them both a wide smile. "I'll save you a place," LuAnn told her as she collected her silverware and carried her well-laden plate away from the serving table.

Kerri nodded, pleased that she would be sitting with her—and with Derrick. It would give them a chance to talk, she thought. Somehow she had to make him understand that she wanted to date him too, and that he shouldn't be angry at her because of Myron.

Once the guests' dishes had been filled, Kerri, Josie, Sandy and Lucille moved into line with Les, Perry and Myron, ready to fill their own plates and relax for a few minutes. Kerri found herself uncomfortably caught between Sandy and Myron.

"Did you two have a nice ride?" Sandy asked suggestively.

"Long," Myron answered. "Definitely a very long ride."

"Saddle-sore?" Kerri teased.

"You come sit with me, and when the music starts after dinner, I'll show you who is saddle-sore," Myron answered, taking her arm as they both turned away from the serving table and looked around at the available spaces.

LuAnn and Derrick were nowhere to be seen in the throng, but Les was waving from a distant table, and Kerri found herself being steered in that direction. Unable to protest, she was soon sitting at the table with the two young men. "Now," Myron said, "suppose you tell me what you've been grinning about ever since we got back."

"Donna is coming two days early," Kerri answered.

"Is that it! I thought it was because we were going to have such a terrific time tonight."

Kerri giggled, unable to resist him. "I didn't know that," she informed him. "What are we going to do?"

Myron winked at Les. "See, it gets them every time," he told him. "No yes-or-no stuff, just make them curious and you'll always have a girl on your arm."

"What are you going to do?" Les asked.

"Wait and see," Myron answered, turning his attention to his plate. "I'll give you both the details later."

"When he decides what they are," Kerri said slyly.

Les joined in her laughter, shaking his head. "You just may have met your match, Myron," he teased. "I think she's already got you figured out."

The teasing and laughter continued as several more of the latecomers joined them. It wasn't till she got up to go to the table for peach cobbler that Kerri caught sight of LuAnn and Derrick on the far side of the terrace. Feeling guilty, she crossed to their table.

"I'm sorry I didn't get to eat with you," she said. "I looked around, but I didn't see you in the crowd. I've got some really neat news. My friend Donna is going to come Tuesday, so she'll have a couple of extra days here."

"It will be nice to meet her," Derrick said politely, his expression blank. He pushed his empty dessert plate to one side. "Ready to go, LuAnn?" he asked.

"Aren't you going to stay for the dancing?" Kerri asked.

"We have things to do at home," Derrick replied. "See you around." He was gone without a backward glance.

Kerri stared after him for several minutes before she went to get her dessert. Now she had no appetite for it. Myron and Les were waiting with several of the guests, but her heart was no longer in their easy bantering. She was relieved when she could excuse herself to go and call Donna.

What was wrong with her? she asked herself as she waited for the call to be completed. Myron was everybody's dream date, and she was fretting over Derrick. It was dumb. She was glad that Donna would soon be with her. Her presence would surely make everything better.

Buoyed up by such thoughts, Kerri returned to the terrace and the dancing. She decided to concentrate on making plans with Myron for the days when Donna would be visiting. If Derrick didn't want to have anything to do with her, she could certainly manage to stay out of his way, she told herself. Myron would be only too glad to help her, she was sure.

Her firm resolve carried her through the weekend, the moonlight steak fry, the boat cruise—now all familiar and less exciting. She was pleased to think that the following week she would be sharing them with Donna.

She saw Myron only during working hours, and Derrick only briefly when she helped serve at the steak fry. She longed to talk to LuAnn about him, but hesitated for fear of making things worse.

The train from Spokane was late and Kerri was nearly beside herself with excitement when Donna finally stepped down from it. "Over here," she shouted, racing past the tourists crowding the platform. "Donna, over here."

The girls hugged each other, then stepped back almost shyly. "You streaked your hair," Kerri gasped.

"Do you like it?"

"It is sensational!"

"Mom about killed me when I came home with it done, but now she likes it. Suzie did it for me. She's practicing to go to beautician school after she graduates next year."

"It makes you look older," Kerri assured her. "Is this all your luggage?" she asked, picking up one of the suitcases.

"I can only stay ten days." Donna's familiar grin erased Kerri's initial feeling of strangeness. "Nine really, since the train leaves about noon on Thursday."

"At least we have a couple of extra days," Kerri told her, leading her toward the waiting station wagon. "Bob's meeting some guests from Seattle," she continued, "so we have to wait a few minutes. Did you have fun on the trip?"

"It was okay," Donna said. "I spent most of my time up in the dome car. There were some kids up there singing and everything."

"It must have been kind of strange . . . coming here alone, I mean."

"I'm here now," Donna said with a grin. "Now tell me everything you've been doing. Are you still dating Myron?"

"I haven't been out since weekend before last," Kerri admitted. "I've been working mostly, trying to get in lots of extra hours so I'd have more free time with you. And we've been making plans . . ." She launched into a description of the various activities she'd discussed with Myron, Les and Perry, finishing, "The only trouble is, I have to work tomorrow afternoon—Both Sandy and Josie have appointments they'd already made before I knew you were coming. There is a ride, though, so you can have fun with Derrick and LuAnn."

"Derrick. You dated him once, didn't you?" Donna asked. "Before Myron, I mean."

Kerri nodded, wanting to tell Donna all about her confused feelings, but unsure how to start. "He's really nice," she told her, noting Bob's approach with a small group of people. "A lot of fun."

There would be plenty of time later to talk. Right now she had to meet the new guests and do her best to help Bob make them and Donna feel welcome.

To her relief, Donna seemed to fit into the group with ease. Both Les and Perry treated her with the friendly, teasing attention they showed to any teenage girl guests, and Donna responded happily. Lucille and Josie welcomed her, though Sandy seemed more reserved, especially after Myron flirted with Donna a little.

After dinner, when things quieted down and they'd returned to her room to get ready for bed, Kerri had time to listen as Donna told her all about the friends she'd left behind. Listening was a bittersweet experience, reminding her of all she'd left in Spokane; yet at the same time, it suffered a little in contrast to the more exciting experiences she'd had since she arrived in Whitefish.

"You're really the lucky one," Donna told her. "I can't imagine dating anyone as exciting as Myron. He's so nice and friendly, too, not at all conceited. I'll bet he could get a date with any girl in the area."

Kerri nodded, remembering Denise. "They fight over him."

"Don't you get jealous?" Donna asked. "I mean, when that girl came over after dinner and was asking him about playing tennis . . ."

Kerri laughed. "I never really thought about it," she admitted. "I mean, playing tennis with the guests is part of his job. I play with them sometimes too, if they need me. But I'm not really good enough to give most of them the kind of game they want."

"I'd be green every time he talked to anyone else," Donna confided. "In fact, I get butterflies when I think about Bruce at home. I mean, what if he goes out with someone while I'm gone?" She lifted the chain that held his class ring, displaying it. "I'd just die if we broke up now. We've only been going together a week."

"You're going steady?" Kerri gasped. "You didn't even tell me!"

Donna giggled. "Mom won't let me go steady, but we've been dating ever since your farewell party and, well, we just like to be together. He's just so special, Kerri," Donna finished, then looked away. "Of course, he's not like Myron, but . . ."

A tap on the door interrupted them, and Kerri's mother peered around the door. "Are you two going to talk all night?" she asked.

Kerri looked guiltily at the alarm clock, which was edging toward eleven thirty. "Are we bothering you?" she asked.

"No, I just thought you might like some cocoa to lubricate your throats after all that talking. And there is still some popcorn left over. Want to come out?"

Kerri agreed. She didn't really want to talk to Donna about the intimacies of dating. When they'd parted, she felt that they were speaking the same language, but now she sensed that her friend had experienced something different and she wasn't ready to think about that yet.

Wednesday morning passed quickly, with Donna accompanying Josie and Kerri as they worked their way through the guest rooms after breakfast. "This doesn't seem too hard," Donna observed.

"It isn't hard," Kerri agreed, "but it goes on all day. As soon as we put this stuff away, we have to go help Mrs. O'Roarke set up for lunch. After lunch we clean up, and then sometimes we have things to do."

"Like what?" Donna asked.

"Well, someone always has to go on the ride to help Derrick and LuAnn. Les works with the boats, renting them out, keeping them repaired. Perry and Myron work on the grounds or Myron plays tennis. We organize picnics, set up card games or supervise swimming parties. Someone has to meet the planes or trains when there are guests coming in. Then there is dinner, and in the evening when the rest of the kids have gone home, I still help out with the evening activities."

"Poor child," Josie teased. "Of course, we stay for the weekly dance, and we'll be around for the campfire tonight. We also stay late for the moonlight ride and steak fry. We stay for anything that Mr. Harriman asks us to."

Donna shook her head. "It really sounds complicated," she admitted. "Are you going to have much time to do things with me, Kerri?"

"After tomorrow I will," Kerri assured her. "I'll still have the housekeeping to do and I'll be serving all the meals, but I'll be free most afternoons to go on the rides. And believe me, I'm looking forward to that."

"Do you want me to wait till you can go?" Donna asked. "I could go swimming this afternoon."

"Oh no, you don't," Kerri said. "I don't want you to miss a single ride on my account. I'll take you down to the stable after lunch myself. I want to introduce you to Derrick and LuAnn and help you pick just the right horse."

Everything went with amazing smoothness until Kerri and Donna reached the corral after lunch. A half dozen horses were already tied outside the corral, dozing in the sun as they waited to be brushed and saddled for the ride. Donna hurried to the corral fence to gaze at the horses beyond it, while Kerri looked around.

"They must be in the stable," she said. "I'll go see. You pick the horse you think you might like."

It was dim in the stable, and it was several minutes before Kerri located LuAnn near the rear of the building. "What's up?" she asked, peering into the stall. "Where's Derrick?"

"Oh, hi." LuAnn looked up from the horse's leg she was bandaging. "Dancer got kicked and it was bleeding pretty badly, so I thought I'd better bring him in and bandage it. Will you tell Mr. Harriman? He might want to have the vet check it."

Kerri nodded. "I hope it isn't serious," she said. "He's a nice horse."

"Somebody put him in the same corral with Comet, and they just hate each other, no one knows why. They get along all right in the pasture, but put them in a small space like a corral and pretty soon the fight starts."

Kerri shook her head, wondering if she'd ever learn everything she needed to know about the horses.

Then she remembered that Donna was waiting. "I just brought Donna down to meet you and Derrick," she explained. "I can't go on today's ride, so I wanted to make sure that she didn't feel too alone."

"I'll be right out," LuAnn said, checking the bandage and patting the horse. "Did you talk to Derrick about a horse?"

"I didn't see him," Kerri said.

"He was in the corral, catching the horses for today." LuAnn emerged from the stall and led the way back out into the sunshine. She stopped in the doorway. "Maybe you didn't see him," she observed, "but it looks like he saw your friend."

Kerri caught her breath sharply as she looked across the corral to see Derrick's dark head bent toward Donna. Donna was looking up at him with a glance that could only be called adoring. For just a heartbeat, Kerri hated her; then sanity returned and she forced a laugh, well aware of LuAnn's watching eyes.

"Guess I won't have to worry about her being lonely," she observed none too happily.

"Let's go see what horse he wants for her," LuAnn suggested.

Kerri looked at her watch. "I guess I'd better go now," she said. "I have to get back to kitchen patrol—I just slipped out to bring Donna down."

"Well, don't worry about her," LuAnn counseled, heading for the corral. "See you at the campfire tonight."

"See you," Kerri called after her, then made her way back toward the lodge, only too conscious of Donna's giggle as it rose on the warm air behind her. All at once she felt sad. She couldn't even look back or wave at Donna. Yet why should it bother her that Derrick obviously found Donna attractive? Didn't she want her best friend to have a good time? Besides, wasn't she dating the handsome and golden-haired Myron? What difference did it make to her what gentle, dark Derrick did?

11

Throughout the long afternoon, Kerri did her best to keep busy. She played a little tennis with one of the women who didn't ride, then spent an hour on the shore watching three children as they played in the water.

Myron joined her on the sand in the late afternoon, wiping perspiration from his deeply tanned face. "Next time I'm going to get the wood ready for the campfire early." He groaned. "Now I remember why boy scouts are always tired."

Kerri laughed at him easily. "Heavy ax?" she asked unsympathetically.

"Chopping wood is harder than peeling potatoes," he said with a grin. "How is Donna getting along?"

"She's gone on the ride," Kerri answered, checking her watch. "I expect they'll be back pretty soon now."

"I think we ought to plan on going into town tomorrow night," Myron suggested. "She should see

Dickerson's and The Rock Around. And Friday and Saturday nights are both busy here, with the moonlight ride and the barbecue.''

"Sounds fine to me," Kerri agreed. "Who all will be going?"

"Man of her choice," Myron answered. "Either Les or Perry or Derrick, if she likes him better. They'd most likely all be there, anyway. Not much else to do in Whitefish."

"I'll ask her this evening," Kerri promised, then added shyly, "Thanks, Myron."

"Got to see that the guests have as much fun as the staff," he told her with a grin, then got to his feet. "Guess I'd better get to work again. It's almost time to see if Mrs. O'Roarke has something for me to peel."

Kerri watched him go with a smile, liking him much more than she'd ever thought possible when she'd first met him. In fact, she thought wryly, sometimes she even forgot how wildly attractive he was. Unable to sort out her feelings, she looked around for Mrs. Green to tell her that she had to return to the lodge and would no longer be able to watch the children for her.

Donna came in glowing from the sun and the ride, but there was little time to talk, as Kerri was busy with dinner preparations and Donna was eager to bathe and change for the evening meal. Later, as they escorted the guests to the shore where Myron and Les were already feeding wood to the fire, Kerri got a chance to ask about her day.

"It was super," Donna answered. "Everyone was so nice, and Derrick is really neat, Kerri. I rode right behind him most of the time, and he told me so much about the area and the horses and just everything."

She paused, then added, "He even asked me to go into town with him and his sister tomorrow night. Do you think that would be all right?"

Refusal rose in her throat, and for a moment she considered reminding Donna of the ring she was wearing around her neck. "I'm sure it will be fine," she managed. "Myron has already suggested that we double-date, so why don't you ask Derrick if he'd like to ride along with us?"

"Hey, terrific," Donna said, then added, "It would be less like a real date that way." She touched the tiny mound the ring made under her shirt. "I mean, we know it's just for fun, but I wouldn't want to do anything that Bruce wouldn't approve of."

"You check with Derrick and let me know," Kerri told her, rushing like one of the guests. "Be right back."

It was nearly half an hour before she could join Donna at the campfire where she and the rest of the guests were toasting marshmallows and listening to Bob and Perry as they played guitars and sang softly. "I didn't know your stepfather was so talented," Donna whispered as Kerri dropped to the sand beside her.

"Neither did I," Kerri admitted. "This is the first time we've done this."

The guests were invited to join in, and the old songs sounded great on the clear, cool night air. It was several minutes before Kerri remembered to ask about the double date.

Donna shook her head. "He says we'll meet you at Dickerson's," she answered. "LuAnn is going with us, and he said that Myron would probably have some of the other kids to take back to town, anyway. Is that okay?"

"Sure, no problem," Kerri told her, thinking privately that Derrick probably didn't want to be in the same car with her. It was a depressing thought. "Everyone always ends up at Dickerson's anyway."

A touch of depression stayed with her all day Thursday, though everything went well. Sky Writer was fine on the ride, showing no sign of the nervous wildness that had plagued her before. Derrick was friendly enough, though she still missed the special closeness she'd felt with him before she dated Myron.

Getting dressed for their dates was fun, almost like the old times in Spokane when they'd prepared to go somewhere together; yet Kerri was aware of a slight strain between them. Occasionally she caught Donna studying her in an odd way. Or did she imagine it?

It was a relief when they came out to find both Myron and Derrick waiting along with Les and Lucille, who were to ride into Whitefish with Myron and Kerri. To Kerri's discomfort, she found herself longing to trade places with Donna, actually envying her the ride into town with Derrick and LuAnn.

"Why so quiet?" Myron asked after they'd dropped Les and Lucille off at their respective homes. "Something bugging you, Kerri?"

"Just tired, I guess," Kerri answered, aware that it was a lie but unable to put into words what she was feeling.

"Hey, you're going to have to perk up," Myron told her, pulling her close. "I've got a big night planned."

"What do you mean?" Kerri asked. "I thought we were going to Dickerson's, then maybe to The Rock Around for pizza."

"We can do that anytime," Myron informed her, his gray eyes gleaming. "I called a buddy of mine, and he informs me that there is a party at the Weltie's tonight. That is a rare occurrence, believe me, and something not to be overlooked."

"What is the Weltie's?" Kerri inquired uneasily. She had a feeling it was going to be another lake party affair of which her mother and Bob would disapprove.

"Well, Gwen Weltie is a local girl. In fact, she was in my graduating class. She lives with her folks in the fanciest house you ever saw. Anyway, two or three times a year her folks go on a trip, and while they are away, Gwen has a party." He paused as though expecting something, but Kerri could think of nothing to say. "Tonight is the night," he finished with less enthusiasm.

"What about Donna and Derrick?" Kerri asked. "We're supposed to be meeting them at Dickerson's."

Myron sighed. "We will," he answered coolly. "Gwen's parties don't get interesting till much, much later."

"Well, I couldn't go without Donna and Derrick," Kerri began.

"So we'll ask them, but nobody else, understand? These are private parties. I don't think anyone else from the staff was invited."

"Were you invited?" Kerri looked at him curiously.

"By sweet little Gwen herself," Myron answered, then grinned roguishly. "I called her right after I talked to my buddy."

"What makes you think Donna, Derrick and I would be welcome?" Kerri asked.

"By the time we get there, no one will be noticing any new faces in the crowd," Myron assured her as he pulled into the parking lot near Dickerson's. "Half the people there won't even be able to see by then. I mean, Gwen knows how to throw a party. There's a big pool, and the recreation room has everything, including a bar that is well stocked. And there will be enough food to make the resort barbecues look skimpy."

"Don't her parents get upset about the parties?"

"Gwen has them right after they leave. That gives her a week or so to get everything cleaned up or replaced." He laughed. "Last summer some idiot poured something in the pool, and she almost didn't have time to get that fixed. She had to have the pool drained and repainted."

"Oh, Myron, I . . ." Kerri began, trying hard to think of a reason for not attending the party, something that wouldn't make her sound like a prude or a child but would be convincing enough that he'd understand and agree.

"Come on. Forget it for now," he advised, taking her arm and hurrying her toward the drugstore. "Remember, not a word to anyone. Let me talk to Derrick, okay?"

Kerri swallowed hard. "Sure." She agreed unwillingly.

Dickerson's was busy and noisy. Kerri felt more at home there now that she recognized a few of the faces that turned their way. Myron claimed a booth with his usual ease, and they were constantly surrounded by people, though only Donna, Derrick and LuAnn actually joined them. The first few minutes were rather strained as Kerri faced Derrick across the table, but after Myron danced with her, then asked LuAnn to dance, the tension began to subside.

After about half an hour, Derrick asked Kerri to

dance. "Did you ask him to do that?" he inquired as
they moved onto the crowded floor where Myron was
already dancing with Donna and LuAnn was dancing
with a boy Kerri didn't recognize.

"Did I ask who to do what?" she responded,
somewhat taken aback by his expression.

"Ask Myron to dance with LuAnn." His dark eyes
probed at her, forcing her to meet his gaze.

"Of course not," Kerri answered. "Why would I do
that?"

"You mean it was his idea?" Derrick sounded
surprised.

"Myron likes LuAnn," Kerri told him. "He told me
once that he thought she'd be a knockout in a couple
of years. Why shouldn't he dance with her?"

Derrick looked away first, and Kerri sensed that he
was embarrassed by her tone. "Hey, don't get mad,"
he said. "I just didn't want him treating my sister like
a charity case."

"No one would think that," Kerri said. "Look at
her, she's having a great time."

Derrick nodded.

"And not a horse in the place," Kerri added.

Derrick grinned at her, and for just a moment she
had the feeling of warmth and happiness that she had
felt that first evening here with him. Then his expression changed and he frowned down at her. "You
aren't thinking seriously of going to the Weltie party,
are you?" he asked.

"Why not?" Kerri responded, stiffening at the
disapproval in his tone. "Didn't Myron invite you and
Donna and LuAnn?"

Derrick nodded, but there was no happiness in his
face. "There's no way I can take my sister to a party

like that," he said. "Dad would kill us both. That's no place for you or Donna either, Kerri."

"Oh come on," Kerri protested. "What can be so bad?"

"The police raided the one last fall and three people were arrested. I told Myron that I couldn't take LuAnn or Donna there." He paused, then continued. "He said he'd take you both if I felt that way, but Kerri, I really think you should both let me take you back to the resort. If he wants to go, let him, but you just can't—"

Kerri opened her mouth to tell him that she was old enough to make her own decisions on such things, but before she could speak, the record ended and Myron and Donna joined them. "Anybody getting hungry yet?" Myron asked.

Kerri looked over to where LuAnn was still standing talking to Tim, the boy she'd been dancing with. "Let's wait a little longer before we go to The Rock Around," she suggested; then looked at Derrick, whose gaze had followed hers. He nodded, seeming to understand her meaning.

"No hurry," Myron said. "I mean, if I pass out from hunger, it shouldn't take more than a couple of guys to carry me out."

"If you pass out from starvation, it will be a miracle," Kerri told him. "I saw your plate at dinner."

"Did you ever notice how cruel girls can be?" Myron asked no one in particular. "Vicious, unfeeling creatures—How come we love them all so much?"

The music began again, a fast number that took all Kerri's concentration as Myron began trying new steps once again. Later, Tim and LuAnn joined them in the booth. Myron suggested pizza again. This time no one objected.

Kerri had expected a chance to talk to Myron about the private party while on the drive to The Rock Around, but Myron had invited four boys to join them on the short trip, so there was no opportunity to do more than laugh at their clowning. Entering the restaurant as the only girl in a group of five boys brought plenty of stares, and Kerri was glad when the other boys left them at the table with Derrick, Donna, LuAnn and Tim.

Once again Myron seemed to have forgotten the party, for he did nothing to hurry the evening, and it was nearly midnight before he brought it up again. "Have you talked to Donna about going to Gwen's party?" he asked as they danced on the crowded floor.

Kerri shook her head. "I haven't had a chance," she admitted. "You can't talk about anything in here. The music is too loud."

"Well, we should be leaving pretty soon, and Derrick isn't going, he told me that." His tone was completely neutral, but Kerri was very conscious of his gaze. His gray eyes were unreadable.

"I'll talk to her as soon as we get back to the table," Kerri promised, suddenly cold despite the heat of the room.

During the next break in the music Kerri suggested that Donna accompany her to the ladies' lounge. It was surprisingly quiet after the deafening music outside, and Kerri leaned against the wall to enjoy the peace for a moment. "Something wrong?" Donna asked.

"Did Derrick tell you about the private party Myron wants to take us to?" Kerri asked.

Donna nodded, her blue eyes troubled. "He says they're awful wild. He won't take me or LuAnn there, but he said if I wanted to go with you and Myron, it was up to me."

"Do you want to go?" Kerri asked.

Donna looked away from her. "Would you hate me if I said no?" she asked. "I mean, you can still go. I'll tell your mother that Myron had made special plans and that you'll be home later."

Kerri studied the pattern in the floor tile intently. She barely saw the bright mosaic of colors. She was remembering the lake party and how she'd felt. She knew with chilling honesty that she hadn't belonged there and that she wouldn't fit into this party either.

"Don't you want to go?" Donna asked, forcing her to look up.

Kerri sighed. "No," she admitted. "They'll be drinking and everything and it's already pretty late. Mom would have a fit if you came home without me and . . . she'd be right."

"What about Myron?" Donna asked.

Kerri shrugged. "He can go if he wants to."

"Without you?" Donna was obviously shocked.

Kerri remembered what she'd heard about the lake party. "They're his friends, Donna," she said. "They'll be going away to school with him in the fall. I won't."

"But—" Donna began. But before she could go on, the door opened and LuAnn peered inside.

"The ice cream you ordered is melting," she informed them. "You'd better come out now or you'll be drinking it."

Kerri went out feeling sure that Myron would reject her and send her home with Derrick like the child he probably thought she was. However, he said nothing after she shook her head in answer to his questioning glance. Only later, on the dance floor did he ask, "Donna decided not to go?"

"And I'm going to have to refuse too, Myron," Kerri replied, meeting his glance. "It's getting late, and after our last date—"

"What time do you have to be home?" he asked.

"About half an hour."

"One more dance, then." He pulled her close, and Kerri surrendered to the excitement and pleasure of being in his arms. Whatever Myron felt, it was obvious that he wasn't angry with her, and at the moment, that was all that mattered.

The mood of understanding lingered even after they left The Rock Around. Kerri felt pleasantly relaxed as she rode along, her head resting on Myron's shoulder. Still, she couldn't help wondering what he was thinking. As they neared the resort, she said, "I'm sorry about the party tonight."

"There will be other parties," he told her, hugging her close as he pulled into the parking lot beside Derrick's family car. He switched off the motor, turned and kissed her in a manner that set her head spinning. "Plenty more," he repeated, then walked her to the kitchen door, where Derrick and Donna were already saying good night.

"See you tomorrow," Kerri whispered.

"Saturday," he corrected. "Tomorrow is my day off."

A moment later Donna and Kerri were inside

alone. Kerri stood at the door, staring at Myron's retreating form. She felt abandoned.

"Is everything all right between you two?" Donna asked. "He isn't mad about tonight, is he?"

Kerri shrugged. "I'm really not sure," she said. "And I don't really know why."

12

In spite of Kerri's doubts, the weekend passed easily enough. Myron never mentioned the party she had refused. Still, Kerri was sad. In her moments of honesty, she knew that Myron was not the cause.

She found that she was miserable riding behind Derrick and Donna as they talked and laughed on the moonlight ride. She disliked even more seeing them together on the deck of the *Lake Belle*. She realized that while she didn't really care too much whether Myron had gone to Gwen's party after he brought her home, she cared desperately that Derrick seemed to enjoy spending time with Donna.

She kept her feelings hidden from Donna as best she could, well aware that it wasn't her friend's fault. She thought she had hidden her feelings until Donna's last day at the resort, when Josie suddenly asked her as they walked toward the cabin, "Did you and Donna have a fight?" Josie asked.

"Heavens, no. Why?" Kerri felt a pang of guilt.

"I don't know. You seem to be sort of cool to each other. She . . . well, she asked me if you were fighting with Myron or something."

"Donna talked to you about me?" Kerri was shocked.

"She's feeling kind of bad," Josie continued. "She says she knows something is wrong, but you won't talk to her. Is something going on, Kerri?" The green eyes were full of friendly concern, stopping any feeling of resentment Kerri might have felt.

Sadness washed over her. "It isn't Donna," she said. "It's me."

They walked in silence for several minutes, then Josie sighed. "Derrick?"

Kerri stopped. "What made you ask that?" she demanded, facing the older girl.

Josie shrugged. "You don't seem to care that Sandy is after Myron again, but Donna has been spending a lot of time with Derrick and you've been watching them like a hawk."

Kerri opened her mouth to deny Josie's suggestion, but instead of words, a sob came out. Josie put her arm around her. "Hey, what's going on?" she asked. "What happened?"

"I made a stupid mistake." Kerri sobbed. "Derrick hates me and I don't know what to do." She told her the entire story, starting with when Derrick saw her kissing Myron in the kitchen.

"I doubt that Derrick hates you," Josie told her when she finished. "Most likely, he just decided that he couldn't compete with the likes of Myron Fuller. You know how most of the guys are. Even Perry and Les will back off if the girl they're with seems to like Myron."

"So what do I do?" Kerri asked. She felt better already just to have put her feelings into words.

"Well, first I think you should talk to Donna," Josie told her. "She's leaving tomorrow, and you don't want her to go home thinking you don't like her anymore."

"But we never seem to have time," Kerri protested.

"So take time," Josie said. "You're free all day today, aren't you? Ask Mrs. O'Roarke for a picnic lunch, and you and Donna ride off on your own. You know the trails well enough by now; you don't need to go with the guests. Give yourselves the whole day, and I'll bet you find out that you and Donna are still just as close as you were before." Josie paused, then took a tissue from the box in the cart. "Now blow your nose and let's get our work done."

Kerri giggled, and blew heartily. "What about my other problem? What do I do about Derrick?" Her voice sounded muffled from behind the Kleenex.

"That's easy," Josie said. "Talk to him, tell him a little bit about how you feel. I have a hunch that's all he's waiting to hear."

"Oh, I couldn't," Kerri gasped. "I mean, what if he just laughed in my face? What if there's someone else? I'd rather die."

Josie shrugged. "Then I can't help you. You'll have to take that chance."

They reached the cabin and worked in silence, till Kerri broke it to say, "Thanks for telling me about Donna. It would be awful if she went home thinking I didn't like her anymore. I'm hoping she and her whole family will come back later in the summer."

"Friends are too important to lose," Josie agreed.

Things seemed to fall into order once they returned to the resort office. Donna was delighted at the idea of a private ride, and Mrs. O'Roarke packed a lunch that Kerri told her would require a packhorse to carry.

"Where shall we ride?" Donna asked once they'd caught and saddled Buck and Sky Writer.

"How about Bear Meadows?" Kerri suggested. "That's a long ride, but I've never been there and it's supposed to be beautiful."

"Sounds good to me," Donna agreed, then she smiled timidly at Kerri. "I'm really glad you had this idea," she went on. "I mean, I've had a terrific time here, but it seems like, well, like we never have any time to just be together the way we were in Spokane."

"That's what I've felt, too," Kerri began, "and it's my fault." She took a deep breath and launched into a complete recital of what had happened between her and Derrick and how it had affected her relationship with Donna. By the time they were halfway to the trail turnoff, their old closeness had returned.

They rode on up the trail, talking contentedly about boys and love and how you knew it was the real thing. They were nearly at the turnoff when Kerri suddenly noticed a change in Sky Writer. She drew rein at once, stroking the mare's shoulder. It was damp with sweat.

"What's the matter with her?" Donna asked.

Kerri shook her head. "I don't know. She acted this way the last time I was on this trail."

"Is she scared of something?" Donna suggested. "Do you suppose she smells a bear?"

"Bob says there aren't any bears up here anymore," Kerri answered, but she continued to watch the mare closely, her pleasure in the ride ebbing as they made the turn toward the higher trail.

"Do you think we should turn back?" Donna asked. "She's really spooky, Kerri."

"If she's afraid of something here, maybe she'll get

over it if we go all the way to the meadow," Kerri
suggested. "She's a terrific horse, Donna, you know
that. This seems to be the only part of the whole ranch
where she gets weird."

They rode on, both too concerned about the fidget-
ing, dancing horse to enjoy the beauty that appeared
at every break in the marching pines. Sky Writer got
no better, and by the time they finally reached the
deep-green, flower-dotted meadow, she was wet from
head to tail and the reins had rubbed ridges of foam
on her neck.

"I guess I'll have to tie her," Kerri said, looking
around the meadow. "If I turn her loose, we won't see
her till we get back to the resort."

"That's for sure," Donna agreed, shaking her head.
"I've never seen anything like it."

They dismounted, and Kerri turned away for a
moment. "There's a stream over there," she began,
"but I'm afraid to let her drink when she's so—"

The mare's shoulder caught her from behind as Sky
Writer leaped forward, tearing her reins from Kerri's
fingers as Kerri stumbled in trying to keep on her feet
feet. Sky Writer leaped across the high grass, heading
for the trail they'd just left. Kerri started after her,
but before she'd taken more than a dozen steps, the
mare suddenly fell crashing to the ground.

"Oh, no!" Kerri gasped, racing along, her own
bruised side forgotten.

Sky Writer lay still in the grass, and for one terrible
moment Kerri thought she was dead. Then she saw
the black-and-white side rising and falling with the
mare's labored breathing. She dropped to her knees
beside the lovely head.

"Is she badly hurt?" Donna asked, panting as she
ran up.

"I don't know," Kerri answered, forcing herself to look beyond the mare's dark eyes to the slender legs. They were clearly visible in the grass, and though she could see a few drops of blood on her knees, there didn't seem to be any serious damage.

"Are you all right, girl?" Kerri asked, stroking the wet neck. She was relieved to see that the white ring of wildness had vanished from around Sky Writer's one visible eye.

The mare lifted her head enough to sniff at Kerri's knee, but made no effort to move. Kerri looked up at Donna, reading her own fears in her friend's eyes. Had the mare broken her back in the fall?

"What shall we do?" Donna asked.

"Could you find your way back alone?" Kerri asked.

"Sure, but—" Donna began.

"I can't leave her here alone," Kerri told her. "Please bring Bob and Derrick. We have to help her."

Donna nodded. "I'll get them here as fast as I can," she promised, mounting the sturdy buckskin, pausing only long enough to add, "I'm sorry, Kerri."

In a moment, she had disappeared into the pines. Kerri stared after her for a heartbeat, then turned her attention back to the mare, stroking her neck and talking quietly to her.

Sky Writer lay still, her labored breathing easing. She seemed in no pain. She even lifted her head to watch as Kerri loosened the girth and eased the saddle away from her back, pulling out the saddle blanket to wipe the sweat from her side.

That done, Kerri returned to the mare's head, petting her, looking into the dark eyes for some sign of the mare's condition. She finger-combed the thick black-and-white mane, noticing as she did that there was a strange notch in her neck where no hair grew.

"I wish I knew what to do for you," Kerri told her, "I wish I knew if you're badly hurt. It's my fault if you are. I should have let Bob sell you to someone else, someone who wouldn't make you come up here when you're so scared."

The black ears flipped companionably and the long tail swished at the flies that were coming to investigate. Kerri studied the slim hind legs again, then ducked as the heavy tail hit her arm. Suddenly she smiled.

"Your back isn't broken," she told the mare. "You couldn't switch your tail if it was."

Sky Writer looked back at her. Kerri ran her hands over the mare's legs and the side that was visible. Sky Writer watched, not reacting. Kerri dug in the saddlebag that was fastened behind her saddle and found a carrot. She offered the mare a bite, then moved away from her.

Sky Writer rolled up onto her belly, moving slowly, almost cautiously. She seemed about to get up, but then slowly settled back to her side. Kerri's heart sank as she dropped beside the horse's head and fed her the rest of the carrot.

The hours seemed endless. It was well into the afternoon before Kerri heard the distant sound of approaching hoofbeats. She got to her feet at once. Sky Writer got back over on her belly. Though she didn't make any effort to get to her feet, she whinnied a loud greeting. Derrick and Bob came galloping into the meadow.

"How bad is she?" Bob asked, dismounting at once. "Are you all right?"

"I'm fine, but she won't get up," Kerri answered, tears filling her eyes. "She gets that far, then she stops."

"Are her legs all right?" Derrick asked.

"As far as I could tell." Kerri winced as she saw that Bob had his rifle in the holster on his horse's shoulder.

"You shouldn't have been up here with her," Bob told her as he moved around the mare, his hands touching her gently but with authority as he examined her. "I told you she wasn't to be trusted."

"She was terrified," Kerri said. "She's not wild, she . . ." She stopped, then asked, "Is she badly hurt?"

Bob sighed. "I can't really tell till we get her on her feet." He looked at Derrick. "Do you think we can roll her over on her other side? She seems to be lying on a incline, and I want to check her other shoulder and hip for damage."

Sky Writer offered surprisingly little resistance, and the two men began lifting and rolling her first over onto her back, then onto her other side. She lay there for a moment, as though surprised by what had happened, then she scrambled onto her belly and, waveringly, to her feet.

"What happened?" Kerri gasped, unable to believe her eyes as Bob led the mare forward a couple of steps, then examined the side Sky Writer had been lying on.

"She's got a badly wrenched shoulder," Bob said, stepping back. "She can't put much weight on it; that's why she couldn't get up while she was lying on a slant."

"Will she be all right?" Kerri asked.

"She'll be well enough to get rid of," Bob answered.

"No, you can't sell her," Kerri protested, putting her arms around the mare's neck.

"Kerri, if you'd been on her, she could've killed you. She's crazy. You can't trust a horse that goes wild for no reason at all."

"What if she had a reason?" Kerri asked, "What if you knew why she did what she did?"

"What possible reason could she have?" Bob asked, frowning at her.

"Didn't you tell me that your mare was attacked by a bear up here?" Kerri asked, hoping desperately that she was right.

"There aren't any bears here now," Derrick said.

"What was her foal like?" Kerri asked, her eyes still on her stepfather's face.

"A little filly, black and white, I think, but . . ." Bob stopped. "Are you trying to tell me that you think Sky Writer . . ."

Kerri smoothed the mare's mane to one side and pointed to the hairless notch. "You said the foal had been injured on the neck, didn't you?" she asked.

There was a long silence while Bob examined the mare's neck, "I guess it could be the same horse," he admitted. "I bought her from a man in Kalispell, but he could've got her from the vet. I never did ask him what happened to her. But—"

"She's only frightened in this place," Kerri continued.

Derrick nodded thoughtfully. "If she associated this place with losing her mother and being hurt . . . it could be the cause."

Bob sighed. "I guess it does make sense," he admitted.

"So what happens now?" Kerri asked, relief making her knees weak. "How do we get her down?"

"Derrick will have to lead her," Bob said. "You can take his horse. I've got to get back to the lodge."

"I think maybe the two of us should lead her down," Kerri said quietly, turning her gaze to meet Derrick's dark eyes. "If Derrick doesn't mind."

Their eyes locked, and for an endless moment she was afraid that he'd refuse. Then he smiled and it was like a caress. "Sounds good to me," he said. "We can take it nice and slow so she doesn't do any more damage to that shoulder."

Kerri looked at her stepfather and saw the understanding in his eyes. "Okay," he said. "I'll ride on back and tell everybody you're both okay. Donna was worried. She wanted to come back with us." He rode off without a backward glance, leaving them alone in the quiet, sleepy meadow.

Derrick said nothing for several minutes, then he patted the mare's neck. "I'm glad you found out about her and that she's okay," he said. "I just don't know how you figured it out."

Kerri smiled at him. "I had a lot of time to think while I was sitting here with her," she began. "In fact, I've been doing an awful lot of thinking, Derrick, about a lot of things."

"What kind of things?" he asked.

"Like how I made a mistake thinking that I wanted to date Myron," Kerri began. "I mean, he's nice and all, but he's really too old for me."

She held her breath, but Derrick said nothing as he started walking toward the trail, leading the limping mare and his own horse behind him. Kerri watched him, feeling her courage melting away again as the red climbed in her cheeks.

After about twenty steps, he stopped and dropped the horse's reins, then he turned and came back to her. Kerri looked up at him fearfully, not sure what she'd see in his face; then her heart lifted. He put his arms around her slowly, almost cautiously, but when his lips found hers, she knew that it was right.

He held her for a long time, then let her go with a sigh. "We'd better get going," he told her. "We have a long walk down this mountain."

"I don't mind," Kerri whispered. "I don't mind at all."

His arm was warm around her shoulders as they went to get the horses. "Me either," he said. "We've got a lot of plans to make."

Kerri glanced over her shoulder at the limping mare, sure that now everything was going to be all right for her. Sky Writer wasn't afraid anymore, and neither was she. They were misfits no longer. The rest of the summer and the next year stretched ahead full of promise. She was home at last.

Four exciting First Love from Silhouette romances yours for 15 days—_free!_

If you enjoyed this First Love from Silhouette® you'll want to read more! These are true-to-life romances about the things that matter most to you now—your friendships, dating, getting along in school, and learning about yourself. The stories could really happen, and the characters are so real they'll seem like friends.

Now you can get 4 First Love from Silhouette romances to look over for 15 days—absolutely free! If you decide not to keep them, simply return them and pay nothing. But if you enjoy them as much as we believe you will, keep them and pay the invoice enclosed with your trial shipment. You'll then become a member of the First Love from Silhouette℠ Book Club and will receive 4 more new First Love from Silhouette romances every month. You'll always be among the first to get them, and you'll never miss a new title. There is no minimum number of books to buy and you can cancel at any time. To receive your 4 books, mail the coupon below today.

First Love from Silhouette® is a service mark and a registered trademark of Simon & Schuster.

—— This offer expires June 30, 1984 ——

First Love from Silhouette Book Club, Dept. FL-019
120 Brighton Road, P.O. Box 5020, Clifton, NJ 07015

Please send me 4 First Love from Silhouette romances to keep for 15 days, absolutely _free_. I understand I am not obligated to join the First Love from Silhouette Book Club unless I decide to keep them.

NAME_____
(Please print)

ADDRESS_____

CITY_____ STATE_____ ZIP_____

Signature_____
(If under 18, parent or guardian must sign)

THERE'S NOTHING QUITE AS SPECIAL AS A FIRST LOVE.

$1.75 each

- 2 ☐ GIRL IN THE ROUGH Wunsch
- 3 ☐ PLEASE LET ME IN Beckman
- 4 ☐ SERENADE Marceau
- 6 ☐ KATE HERSELF Erskine
- 7 ☐ SONGBIRD Enfield
- 14 ☐ PROMISED KISS Ladd
- 15 ☐ SUMMER ROMANCE Diamond
- 16 ☐ SOMEONE TO LOVE Bryan
- 17 ☐ GOLDEN GIRL Erskine
- 18 ☐ WE BELONG TOGETHER Harper
- 19 ☐ TOMORROW'S WISH Ryan
- 20 ☐ SAY PLEASE! Francis

$1.95

- 24 ☐ DREAM LOVER Treadwell
- 26 ☐ A TIME FOR US Ryan
- 27 ☐ A SECRET PLACE Francis
- 29 ☐ FOR THE LOVE OF LORI Ladd
- 30 ☐ A BOY TO DREAM ABOUT Quinn
- 31 ☐ THE FIRST ACT London
- 32 ☐ DARE TO LOVE Bush
- 33 ☐ YOU AND ME Johnson
- 34 ☐ THE PERFECT FIGURE March
- 35 ☐ PEOPLE LIKE US Haynes
- 36 ☐ ONE ON ONE Ketter
- 37 ☐ LOVE NOTE Howell
- 38 ☐ ALL-AMERICAN GIRL Payton
- 39 ☐ BE MY VALENTINE Harper
- 40 ☐ MY LUCKY STAR Cassiday
- 41 ☐ JUST FRIENDS Francis
- 42 ☐ PROMISES TO COME Dellin
- 43 ☐ A KNIGHT TO REMEMBER Martin
- 44 ☐ SOMEONE LIKE JEREMY VAUGHN Alexander
- 45 ☐ A TOUCH OF LOVE Madison
- 46 ☐ SEALED WITH A KISS Davis
- 47 ☐ THREE WEEKS OF LOVE Aks
- 48 ☐ SUMMER ILLUSION Manning
- 49 ☐ ONE OF A KIND Brett
- 50 ☐ STAY, SWEET LOVE Fisher
- 51 ☐ PRAIRIE GIRL Coy
- 52 ☐ A SUMMER TO REMEMBER Robertson

First Love from Silhouette

53 ☐ LIGHT OF MY LIFE Harper

54 ☐ PICTURE PERFECT Enfield

55 ☐ LOVE ON THE RUN Graham

56 ☐ ROMANCE IN STORE Arthur

57 ☐ SOME DAY MY PRINCE Ladd

58 ☐ DOUBLE EXPOSURE Hawkins

59 ☐ A RAINBOW FOR ALISON Johnson

60 ☐ ALABAMA MOON Cole

61 ☐ HERE COMES KARY! Dunne

62 ☐ SECRET ADMIRER Enfield

63 ☐ A NEW BEGINNING Ryan

64 ☐ MIX AND MATCH Madison

65 ☐ THE MYSTERY KISS Harper

66 ☐ UP TO DATE Sommers

67 ☐ PUPPY LOVE Harrell

68 ☐ CHANGE PARTNERS Wagner

Coming in December . . .
NEED A GOOD LAUGH? read
SEND IN THE CLOWNS
by Marilyn Youngblood

FIRST LOVE, Department FL/4
1230 Avenue of the Americas
New York, NY 10020

Please send me the books I have checked above. I am enclosing
$_____ (please add 75¢ to cover postage and handling. NYS and NYC residents please add appropriate sales tax). Send check or money order—no cash or C.O.D.'s please. Allow six weeks for delivery.

NAME _____

ADDRESS _____

CITY _____ STATE/ZIP _____

15-Day Free Trial Offer
6 Silhouette Romances

6 Silhouette Romances, free for 15 days! We'll send you 6 new Silhouette Romances to keep for 15 days, absolutely free! If you decide not to keep them, send them back to us. You pay nothing.

Free Home Delivery. But if you enjoy them as much as we think you will, keep them by paying the invoice enclosed with your free trial shipment. We'll pay all shipping and handling charges. You get the convenience of Home Delivery and we pay the postage and handling charge each month.

Don't miss a copy. The Silhouette Book Club is the way to make sure you'll be able to receive every new romance we publish before they're sold out. There is no minimum number of books to buy and you can cancel at any time.

This offer expires June 30, 1984

 Silhouette Book Club, Dept. SF2273
120 Brighton Road, Clifton, NJ 07012

Please send me 6 Silhouette Romances to keep for 15 days, absolutely free. I understand I am not obligated to join the Silhouette Book Club unless I decide to keep them.

NAME _____

ADDRESS _____

CITY _____

STATE _____ ZIP _____